Like, Follow, Kill

CARISSA ANN LYNCH

OneMoreChapter

One More Chapter
a division of HarperCollins*Publishers* Ltd
1 London Bridge Street
London SE1 9GF

www.harpercollins.co.uk

This paperback edition 2019

First published in Great Britain in ebook format by
HarperCollins*Publishers* 2019

A catalogue record for this book
is available from the British Library

ISBN: 9780008362645

This novel is entirely a work of fiction.
The names, characters and incidents portrayed in it are
the work of the author's imagination. Any resemblance to
actual persons, living or dead, events or localities is
entirely coincidental.

Typeset in Birka by Palimpsest Book Production Ltd,
Falkirk, Stirlingshire

Printed and bound in the UK

This book is dedicated to my editor, Charlotte Ledger, and my agent, Katie Shea Boutillier. Thank you both for believing in my stories and making me a better writer.

Always eyes watching you and the voice enveloping you. Asleep or awake, indoors or out of doors, in the bath or bed—no escape. Nothing was your own except for the cubic centimeters in your skull.

George Orwell, 1984

I was born with a scream inside me. Lodged between my heart and throat. Can't swallow it; can't choke it down. Can't spit that motherfucker out. It's stuck, like me … anchored to the in-between, slowly rotting in the core of me. It festers like a sore, oozing through my bloodstream, sending seeping shocks of silent fury to every nerve ending in my body.

Like an IV, it drip, drip, drips, but there's never a release.

One of these days, I'll open my mouth and the world will rumble from the roar.

Chapter 1

*M*y body is broken.

Arms like dying, desperate fish, they flop on the seat beside me. Hips yanked from their sockets. Red-rose gashes on my chest and neck.

A deep dark hole where my nose once was.

And my teeth ... these teeth don't belong to me. Like broken eggshells, they stab the roof of my mouth, pricking my cheek and gums.

Are they Chris's teeth?

If so, how did Chris's pearly white, now-broken teeth end up in my mouth? Did I kiss him?

No, not a kiss.

I can't remember the last time I kissed him ... but I can taste his blood in my mouth.

Chris with the cocoa-colored eyes and hair like silk on my skin. Chris with the lips, soft as falling feathers on a windy day ...

Chris: the love of my life.

Chris: who is dead.

1

One minute we were laughing ... *or were we shouting?* Discussing our plans for the day ... although now I've forgotten what those plans were.

And the next ... *the next* ... we're upside-down, strapped in our seats like a rollercoaster, only we can't get off, we're stuck, suspended in mid-air. The roof of my Buick becomes the sky. I'm mesmerized as it swirls like one of those psychedelic spinning tunnels, like they have at the county fair.

Oh, the fair. That's where we were going, weren't we?

Chris promised me a deep-fried Snickers bar.

And I promised him I'd stay sober.

Chris: The Love Of My Life and Chris: The Headless Man On The Seat Beside Me are one and the same.

This is my fault.

Chris is dead.

I did this.

I. Did. This.

I stopped answering my phone months ago, but that didn't stop my sister from calling. Every day, at five past noon—a phantom phone call, followed by a buzzing barrage of texts.

Hannah is calling ... read my phone screen.

But Hannah was always calling. And I, her less attractive, less successful, less *stable* sister, was always ignoring those calls.

As predicted, the texts came next:

Hannah: How are you today? Want to go out to lunch? Need me to stop by?

Translation: *Are you alive? When are you going to do normal things again? Don't tell me I need to come over there and drag you out of bed again.*

Me: Busy. Can't. No.

My sister is more than my sister. She practically raised me after the death of our mother.

I would love nothing more than to answer her calls, to have her beside me—but not this version of her. Not the sister that tiptoes around me like I'm a melting chunk of ice in the center of a deep, black sea.

I'm a sinking ship she wants to save ... but she's too afraid to come aboard. Because, deep down, she knows I'll suck her into the murky black hole, too, just like I did with Chris.

Wiggling my jaw, I tried to ease the phantom tooth pains as I pulled myself out of my twin-sized bed. The sheets and comforter lay tangled at my feet. Angry red numbers blinked at me from the clock on my bedside table. It was 12:30 in the afternoon, the time when most normal people were working.

Everything hurt: my arms, legs, chest, and back. *My teeth.*

Traces of the dream still lingered and would stay there for most of the day, the way they always did.

My nightstand was covered in pill bottles. I twisted the caps off, one by one, and swiped out two pills of each. Pain pills. Anxiety meds. Leftover antibiotics. Another med to counter the side-effects of the first two. I washed them down with an ashy can of Mountain Dew. Grimaced.

3

Every night, the same thing: the car accident reenacted, but the details were always fuzzy, always evolving ... whether the actual memories of that night were becoming lucid or more convoluted, was unclear.

I just wish they'd go away. Period.

It's not that I don't want to think about Chris. I miss him ... I love him ... but I can't.

I can't let myself go back to that place. I'm Hannah's sinking ship, and Chris ... well, Chris is mine.

No, dear husband, I will not come aboard.

Because if I do, if I let myself go there ... that ship will suck me down, down, down, and never let me loose.

During my wakeful hours, I'd become an expert at burying my feelings. But these dreams—these warped flashbacks of the accident—were trying to remedy that all on their own. I could push away the memories and the horrors while I was awake, but when I closed my eyes ... the dreaming side of myself took control. That side of myself wouldn't allow me to forget, no matter how much I wanted to.

Maybe it's payback for what I did.

Karma.

What goes around comes around—isn't that how the saying goes?

For the rest of my life, will I have to relive those awful, ticking moments in that crushed-up Buick?

Of all the things about me that needed fixing, the sleep/dream issue was my priority. But my doctor wouldn't prescribe sleep medication, or any other downers. They didn't mix well with my other meds.

I want to be reassembled. Scrapped for parts. My memories wiped clean.

I padded down the hallway to the bathroom, leaving my buzzing phone behind. Without turning on the bathroom light, I began my lonely morning ritual in the dark— brushing my teeth, gargling mouthwash, combing the knots from my hair.

The dream snaked its way back into my brain while I brushed.

Cringing, I recalled the gummy taste of my own teeth. The teeth that I had initially—and strangely—believed to be my husband's teeth.

I can still taste blood in my mouth. But whose blood is it? It's like sucking on a battery dipped in sugar.

Taking a deep breath, I flicked the light switch on before giving myself a chance to change my mind.

My toothbrush fell from my mouth, bouncing in the sink, as I studied my reflection in the bathroom mirror. No matter how many times I saw my face, I'd never get used to it now.

I look worse than the last time I checked.

It looked like someone was pinching my nose, the bridge a hard knot in the center of my face, the nostrils squished flat on both sides. The plastic surgeon had done the best possible job.

There's only so much we can do, Camilla …

The skin on my nose was darker, which made sense—it didn't belong to me. Ten surgeries and counting. So far—two to "repair" my nose using someone else's skin and cartilage, four to fix my broken teeth with mostly false ones, and another four to fix my legs. My hips hadn't been pulled from their sockets, but it sure had felt that way at the time. But both legs had been broken, one worse than the other, and now two metal rods and countless screws resided inside me, extending from my shin bones all the way to the top of my thighs. My wrist had been sprained. My elbow shattered.

My heart smashed to bits.

I was beautiful once. Chris used to say so. Until my reckless driving had led us to the backend of a flatbed truck. *Oh, what I wouldn't give to hear the gravelly shake of his voice … to see that one eyebrow flexing playfully as he tucked my always-messy brown hair behind my ears …*

You're the most beautiful girl I ever did see: his words.

We hadn't been upside down either, like the dream implied—another figment of my twisty reinterpretation of what actually happened that night. The car was crushed beneath the semi's trailer, my whole world spinning like a top because that's what happens when you have a concussion.

A big chunk of my nose was severed by windshield glass. And Chris … he'd lost more than his nose. His death was horrific. *He didn't deserve to die that way.*

Splashing icy cold water on my face, I forced myself

not to think of him. Deep down, I knew that if I gave in to that craving ... to think about Chris, to go back in my mind to how things used to be ... that it would become an obsession.

If I think too long and hard about Chris, I may never stop.

The anxiety pills helped with the flashbacks while I was awake.

It's like there's this version of me, living inside my head, and once the meds kick in, I can hear her in the corner, her voice murky and low ... she's scared, she's worried, she's ashamed ... but then the pills flood my bloodstream and her voice gets drowned out completely. I imagine her in there somewhere, floating in the lazy river of my bloodstream, wondering when I'll let her back out. The numbness never lasts—drugs help, but they can't alleviate my misery. They can't cure loneliness, either.

Sometimes that girl drifts so far downstream, I don't think I'll ever reach her again ...

I flipped the light switch back off, the sudden change in lighting causing a sharp twinge in my right temple. The head pains often came and went so quickly, almost like they were a figment of my imagination.

I liked leaving every light in the house off and the shutters closed until darkness came, and I was forced to illuminate myself and my surroundings.

But one light in the house was always shining—the glare from my laptop computer. It beckoned me from my desktop in the living room.

7

Now, here is an addiction I can handle, and sometimes, control.

I turned on the coffee pot in the kitchen then sat down in front of my computer, a rushing wave of relief rolling through me. This was my life now—the internet, my only window to the outside world.

Lucky for me, it's a pretty large window.

A lonely window, but a window, nevertheless …

"I wonder where we're going today?"

I refreshed my browser from where it had frozen last night and Valerie Hutchens' shiny face blossomed like a milky-white flower across my home screen.

_TheWorldIsMine_26 had over 2,000 posts and nearly 10,000 followers, and like Valerie herself, the Instagram account was growing and improving daily.

"Where are you now, Valerie?" I clicked on her newest Instagram story.

Branson, Missouri.

Straddling this world and the next. #livingmybestlife, her caption told me.

Valerie's hair was different today—her sunny blonde bob had skinny curtains of pale pink on either side of her face. Maroon lips. Kohl-rimmed eyes. A body that was neither fat nor walking-stick thin, just perfect.

Valerie Hutchens is perfect.

In this latest story, she was straddling two train rails, arms spread wide in a V. Her palms were open, fingertips reaching for the sky. Dusty sunlight shimmered through her pale white dress. She had on brown leather boots—the boots she'd bought in Texas three weeks ago, I remembered—so tall they almost reached the hem of her dress.

I could feel the goosebump-inducing burn of the sun on the back of her arms and legs.

She was looking at something overhead, something no one else could see ...

It's like she doesn't care if we're watching. Like she's simply living out loud, while the rest of us sit here in awe of her, just like we did back then.

But technically, that wasn't true. If Valerie didn't care what people thought, she wouldn't be posting about her travels all day and all night on social media, I reminded myself.

But still, I didn't really believe that either. Valerie operated on her own agenda, independent of everyone else—*she always has.*

I liked her post—I always do—then I flicked the screen off. Next, I forced myself to go shower and make some lunch.

My addiction to Valerie had become so great that I was restricting myself to one check per hour. And believe me, an hour was generous.

Lunch was a sizzling plate of chicken fajitas and spicy black beans.

The best fajita in the whole world lives right here in Branson #nomnom, according to Valerie.

9

It did look tasty—the juicy strips of meat and plump toppings spread out on an iron skillet billowing with steam.

She had changed her clothes since this afternoon.

In a dark back booth, she wore a low-lit smile, in what appeared to be a mostly empty restaurant. She posed for the camera in a lacy black shawl that slipped from her shoulders. If I maximized the screen, I could almost see the constellation of freckles on her right shoulder ... four dots in the shape of a diamond, with a few little dots forming a tail, almost like a Valerie-version of the Little Dipper on her skin.

Her smudgy black makeup from this afternoon was gone, replaced with pale-pink shadow on her lids, no trace of concealer.

Lovingly, Valerie stared down at her plate of fajitas and beans.

Her beauty was inspiring, but also a constant reminder of my own ugliness. My own isolation ...

I can't remember the last time I ate Mexican. Or ate out anywhere for that matter, I thought, slowly chewing my limp cheese-and-mayonnaise sandwich. The cheese had expired two days ago, the edges of the slice slightly stiff. Chewing, I tried not to taste it. My cherry-oak computer desk was littered with soda cans and leftover plates from last night's snacking-while-stalking session.

What a mess. Valerie makes me feel like a total slob. At the same time, I can't stop watching ...

My incision sites on my legs were sore but manageable; the headaches were painful but short-lived. The damage to my face was mostly about vanity ...

The accident had changed me, and the damage was done. But it wasn't so much damage that I couldn't get around, or walk, or even drive for that matter. I had to be careful about driving because of my medication, but the doctor had cleared me anyway, much to my dismay. Ten weeks of physical therapy and now my therapist was *encouraging* me to get out and move more.

I can leave this apartment. I can clean up after myself. I'm capable of so much more ...

But the truth was ... I didn't want to leave. I wasn't ready to face the world, or more specifically, the people in town who knew about the accident. *The accident that I caused.*

I slammed my fists down on the desk on either side of the keyboard, rattling half-empty cans and spilling the contents of a dusty old pencil-holder.

Focus. Focus on what she's doing.

Valerie's newly dyed hair was pulled up into a sloppy ponytail, loose strands of petal pink curling around her face and neck.

I'll never forget the first time I saw her.

Valerie wasn't local; not one of those kids you'd known since grade school, wiping boogers on the back of your seat in first grade, then sporting a Wonderbra in seventh. We didn't know anything about this new girl, not really ...

She came from ... *where was it? Arizona, I think.* Her

11

parents were either dead or deadbeats; she'd moved in with her aunt. She was the 'new girl'.

But to us, it was like she'd stepped off another planet and crashed into our hemisphere without any warning. And without an invitation.

Two weeks into seventh grade—my first year as a middle-schooler at Harmony—the alien showed up at our morning assembly. I was proud of how I looked that year. My breasts had developed into tiny buds that weren't much, but they made me feel good, and I'd worked all summer, doing odd jobs, mostly babysitting, in order to buy six new outfits for school. Designer jeans. Fancy flannel button-ups (they were reversible!). A couple name-brand hoodies. A pair of painfully stiff Doc Martens. White, no-show socks and panties with designs on them that weren't cartoons.

Every morning, I spent no less than an hour making my hair and makeup as flawless as they could possibly get. The only girls I envied were the few who did it better than me—some girls had better clothes, or they didn't have to wear a repeat outfit on week two. Some of the girls had a knack for hair and makeup.

I envied *some*, but not many. I felt good in my skin ... well, I thought I did.

But then the alien showed up, posing as a *girl* named Valerie Hutchens. When she walked into our morning assembly, the envy I felt was instantaneous. It consumed me ...

But what I couldn't understand was *why*.

She was wearing a T-shirt that obviously belonged to her father, or maybe an older brother. *Violent Femmes*, the front of it read, the *es* on the end so faded that I couldn't actually read it, I just knew the band, so I filled in the blanks. The shirt was three sizes too big for her and the crack of her shorts was crooked in the back. No-name shoes without any socks, the laces untied. Tweety Bird panties protruding over the top of her shorts every time she bent over to pick something up.

On that first day, she walked in and took a seat in the first open spot on the bleachers. She smiled at our principal, Mrs. Sauer, and even though Mrs. Sauer *never* smiled, she smiled back at Valerie that day.

I couldn't take my eyes off her as she finger-combed her shiny, shoulder-length blonde hair. Long hair was in style that year at Harmony, or it was supposed to be ... but somehow, Valerie's short, stylish 'do ruined all that—it made me self-conscious of my own long, brown locks, and it wasn't long before the "in style" was nasty tees and short hair and don't-give-a-fuck shoes, because, let's face it, what was really in style was: Valerie Hutchens.

Can I borrow a pencil? she'd asked one of the boys on the seat above her. He fell all over himself scrounging one up. *Keep it,* he said. *I'm Luke.*

Luke was a nerd, so I rolled my eyes. But Valerie didn't—she smiled with all her teeth, not a flirtatious smile but a genuine one, and then busied herself, writing in a black-and-white notebook poised in her lap.

13

What is she writing about? It seemed so stupid, so unimportant, how I felt this urge—this *need*—to know exactly what words she scribbled into that tattered old book of hers. But I never found out; no one did. She kept her writing to herself, just like she kept everything. *She was so available, yet so private at the same time …*

As the school weeks marched on, I learned a few more things about Valerie Hutchens: she was just as nice as she was pretty; she was smart as a whip without even trying; and she was talented in all things extracurricular: volleyball, music, theater, cheerleading, art, you name it. She signed up for everything. And it didn't seem like a ploy to gain popularity, just an actual interest in all things Harmony. The boys followed her around like puppies; the girls wanted to be her friends. And although she was kind to everyone, she was never really close to anyone. Including me.

I admired her from a distance for the next six years as she blossomed into a young adult and carried her magnetism with her into high school. It wasn't until tenth or eleventh grade that I realized why I wanted to be friends with Valerie. It wasn't her talents or her creativity. It wasn't her good looks or the way she lit up a room when she walked inside it. It wasn't even the fact that she was so goddamned nice and likable.

It was the way she didn't give a shit about any of these things.

Valerie Hutchens never laid awake at night, worrying

about what she would wear to school, or who her friends were, or if she'd make the basketball team. Valerie was a floater, freely drifting through life on a fluffy cloud, always living in the here and now.

She had the confidence that I lacked, which is why I wanted to be her friend.

That smile ... I wanted to be on the receiving end of it.

But her eyes floated over me; I might as well have been a ghost, stalking the airless halls of Harmony ...

I would have preferred being hated or mocked ... anything besides ignored.

I watched the others who followed her around—Luke and some of the other nerdy boys. Valerie was too nice to turn them away, too cool to give them a real chance. I wouldn't stoop to their level; I wouldn't grovel for her attention.

Shortly after my accident, memories of Valerie came floating back like they'd never left in the first place. It wasn't until I had managed to get out of bed and venture back online that I thought about the girl from high school. Her perfect face consumed me. I don't know what triggered it—I just woke up one day and wondered if she was on Facebook. Like so many of my other classmates and former friends, I expected her to have a profile where she doted on her husband and kids; maybe occasionally bragged about her Etsy business ... but Valerie didn't have a Facebook profile, much to my surprise.

Apparently, Facebook isn't really that cool anymore among

15

young people. Who knew? I certainly never got the damn memo. But Valerie did. Of course she did.

A few weeks later, I tried searching again. Only this time, I used Google to find her. She hated Facebook, but she was active on Instagram and Snapchat. In fact, she spent more time posting than she did living, or so it appeared at first.

Since finding her profiles, I'd become absorbed in all things Valerie Hutchens.

When Valerie goes to the beach, so do I. I can almost taste the salt of the ocean, hear the whisper of waves in Panama City …

Valerie was a pharmaceutical rep, which meant she traveled for her job—*a lot*, apparently. How ironic, that I was the one choking down the pills while she was the one peddling them.

But that wasn't her only job. She was also an aspiring writer, like me.

Almost done with my first novel. Will you guys read it someday? Please say yes! #amwriting #writerforlife.

It was a black-and-white photo of her sitting on the edge of a pier in Ocean City, Maryland, dangling her toes over the edge, all the while balancing a notebook full of tiny, neat words on her lap. Hell, it could have been the cover of her very own book—that's how good the picture was.

But the photo itself made me nervous—*What if a sudden breeze came rushing by, and her pretty little words floated out to sea?* But, of course, Valerie didn't worry about things like that. Because bad things didn't happen to people like Valerie.

Bad things happened to me.

Look on the bright side, every once in a while, Kid, Chris's words and cheesy smile ripped like blades through my cerebrum.

He was the optimist; I was the realist—and together, we kept each other in check.

But not anymore.

There's no one left to lean on.

I pushed aside thoughts of Chris, focusing only on Valerie.

Maximizing the old picture of her on the pier, I tried to catch a few of her words. But I couldn't make them out. Even now, nearly fifteen years later, I couldn't sneak a peek into Valerie's inner world, no matter how hard I tried ...

My favorite post of Valerie's was one from about a month ago. She was standing outside our old middle school. ***Passing through town again, thought I'd stop and see Aunt Janet! Look where I am! I don't remember much about Harmony, but it feels right being back in Wisconsin. Only back for one day. What should I do? #Imbaaaack #homesweethome #instawisconsin***

She couldn't remember much about Harmony, but one thing was certain: Harmony hadn't forgotten about her. Dozens of people commented on her post, including her old pal Luke, and I recognized some of my other classmates by either their usernames or profile pics. I even recognized our old high-school algebra professor in the comments— young and old alike, everyone worshipped Valerie.

Apparently, I'm not the only one still watching Valerie from a distance.

I felt embarrassed for all the commenters. But most of all, I felt embarrassed for me.

Back pressed to the brick under the Harmony Middle School sign, she had one leg bent, her foot pressed to the wall, both hands casually tucked in her torn jean pockets. I imagined myself sending her a private message—*Just saw that you're in town! This is Camilla Brown. Do you remember me from school? I thought if you weren't busy, we could meet for coffee or drinks. Catch up?*

But of course, I didn't send it. *I'm ashamed to even admit that I practiced writing it.* Even if my fucking face and body weren't twisted and lame, I still didn't think I could face her. I liked her post—the way I always did—then erased the message.

Closing my eyes, I tried to imagine what a meet-up with Valerie would look like.

Do I think she would meet up with me if I asked real nicely? Yes, I do. Because Valerie is polite like that. Valerie is ... well, Valerie. Always charming, always kind, always out of my league ...

When I imagined us sitting across from each other in a local café, chatting away like old friends, I couldn't help picturing my real face—*correction: my old face*—the one I had before the accident.

It wasn't until weeks later, when she was back out on the road, far enough away that it felt safe, that I sent my first message.

She'd responded—it had taken a few days, but still—and since then, we'd chatted briefly. She remembered me from school. She asked me how I was doing. She didn't mention the accident or Chris, so one could only hope she hadn't heard ...

In my messages, I complimented her pictures. I tried to keep it short and sweet, un-desperate.

We talked a little bit about writing, although she still hadn't told me—or any of her other followers—what she was writing, exactly. I didn't mention my face, and I never suggested that we hang out in person. She didn't either ... *perhaps she is waiting for me to suggest it?*

There was no point in trying to see her in person. There weren't going to be any chatty meet-ups.

Because I didn't want to be her friend—*I don't think I ever really wanted to be her friend.*

No, that wasn't it at all.

I didn't want to be on the receiving end of Valerie's smiles, I wanted to wipe them off her pretty face.

Chapter 2

My house smelled of decay. Everything had that dirty-dishrag aroma clinging to it, even me. No matter how much I cleaned or sprayed, the apartment stank.

Maybe it's not the house that's rotten and falling apart. Maybe it's me.

A walking corpse—that's me.

The house was small; so small, I often caught myself calling it my "apartment." Eight hundred rented square feet of mildew-laden carpet; dingy walls the dull color of Cheerios. And not a decoration to speak of.

But I had what I needed to survive—a kitchen, one bathroom, a cramped living room, and a bedroom that could easily be mistaken for a walk-in closet. It was the cheapest thing my sister and I could find for me after the accident. She offered to let me stay in her nice, two-story, brick home in town. But she and I both knew that wasn't an option. Her house was only a few blocks from my old one ... the house I used to share with Chris. And she had her own life, her own family to tend to ...

The drab walls, the isolation ... it was less like an apartment, and more like a prison. *And maybe that's how I want it to be ... a form of self-punishment, I suppose.*

I didn't want to be around anyone after the accident ... *do I now?*

No, not really, I realized.

It helped talking to Valerie online—she was my window to the world. And sure, I was lonely, but the alternative ... being surrounded by people, them judging my face, my mistakes ... loneliness seemed like the better option.

My rental home was on the outskirts of town, with only one neighbor beside me. She was an elderly woman ... *Karen ... or Carol, maybe?* I couldn't remember. Karen/Carol's house was barely visible in the warmer months, a thick tangle of trees forming a wall between us.

My place was cramped, but it was also the most secluded and affordable place for rent in Oshkosh.

When you never leave your 800-square-foot apartment, it actually feels more like 400 square feet.

The walls closing in on me, the distance between the ceiling and floor was shortening by the day, threatening to crush the breath from my chest like one of those X-ray machines they use while performing mammograms ...

My old place with Chris had been nothing like this. I could barely remember the sunny walls of our townhouse or the neat parquet floors throughout. I could barely remember Chris for that matter ... the way he was before ...

But that's a lie.

21

I could still remember *everything*, if I allowed myself to. That old version of me trapped inside my head—she wouldn't let me forget. I could silence her voice, but not her memories. No, some memories never die, no matter how much we want them to.

I want to forget … it's easier to forget a life that I destroyed.

We had a great relationship, Chris and me. Not good, *great*.

I imagined the weight of him, thick hairy arms draped around my neck while I typed at my desk. Chris massaging my shoulders, twisting his fingers through my hair, tugging at the knots … hands squeezing my neck, not so hard I couldn't breathe, but enough to give me pause …

But my life was different now. For the most part, I spent my days reading books and watching TV to keep myself sane. I bathed and exercised (a bit) and cooked food. But the moments between those activities and sleeping, those moments belonged to the internet. Searching and looking … trying to find myself somewhere, I guess. Lately, I'd been consumed by Valerie.

It wasn't her video on Instagram at 2am that woke me, because I was already awake. In the wee morning hours … that was when I often ventured outside, but never beyond the concrete slab I used as a porch.

Perched in a rusty lawn chair, a shapeless cloud of smoke formed around my head like a bubble. Pall Malls—another addiction I couldn't quite master or shake.

Karen/Carol couldn't see me from here, even if she was

looking. But still, I'd left the back porch light off just in case. I didn't want to be seen. Looking at my own scars was hard enough; I didn't need others staring at them, too.

The 2am notification shook me out of my dream-like, smoking state. I stubbed my cigarette out on the rim of an empty soda can on the table beside me, then squinted down at my iPhone. The white-hot brightness of the phone in the dark caused a sharp twinge of pain in my right temple.

_TheWorldIsMine_26 started a live video. Watch it before it ends!

Valerie posted live videos a few times per week, but 2am, even for a frequent poster like her, was unusual. Hours earlier she'd posted several photos on Instagram and a Snapchat story in a smoky underground club in eastern Kentucky called *Cavern*.

Meeting some interesting new ppl in Paducah! Cavern is the best-kept secret here. But it's all about business tonight though. #allworknoplay #hustling

The club had a dingy, dark look to it ... but Valerie herself was dressed to the nines, in a navy-blue suit that made her hair look white hot and glossy in the photos. I noticed the pink strips in her hair were now gone ...

Most likely, she was wining and dining some doctors or other consumers in the healthcare industry. Working that Valerie charm to push whatever the latest drug product on the market was.

I clicked on the newest video, holding my breath in anticipation.

The video was dark, so it was hard to see, and for a moment the screen bumbled and glitched ... then Valerie's nose and lips filled the entire screen.

Immediately, I felt a prickle of fear in my stomach. *Something is wrong.*

"Not a good night, guys. Not a good night at all," Valerie's bow-like lips moved shakily on the screen. They were puffy. Stained purple with drink.

"The meeting was swell, but some creep decided to follow me back to my hotel room. Can you guys stay with me, please ...?" The screen bobbled and shook as she walked; all I could see was the lower half of her face. She was panting, releasing short gulps of air through her swollen lips. And she was stumbling too ... possibly drunk.

I've never seen her this vulnerable.

"Almost there, guys ... thanks for having my back," she huffed. The video panned out and finally, I could see her whole face. Her eyes were wide, more frightened than I'd ever seen them before. And she was surrounded by darkness, spiky dark buildings in the distance, but nothing decipherable. Surely, if she were close to the hotel, there would be lights ... *Speaking of lights, where are all the street lights in that town ...?*

"As much as I love being on my own, sometimes I feel like I need a hero. There are lots of creeps in the world, guys. But I know I'm safe with you all watching, always having my back ..."

The video cut off abruptly.

I gripped the phone, surprised to hear myself panting just like she was seconds earlier.

Will she post again, to let us know that she made it inside safely?

At 4am, I finally climbed into bed. *Should I send her a message, ask her if she's okay?* I was always hesitant to message Valerie, afraid of annoying her or seeming desperate ... but she could be in trouble ...

Ultimately, I decided to wait until morning. *Valerie will be okay, she always is.*

I balanced the phone on my chest. If she posted, my phone would vibrate, and hopefully, wake me up.

I stared at the fan blades ... *swish swish swish* ... until my eyelids grew heavy and closed.

The sound of a phone ringing shook me from sleep. Thankfully, I hadn't dreamed of the accident. I jerked up in bed, trembling for no reason, and immediately, I remembered Valerie's odd live video she'd posted in the middle of the night. *Did she make it back to her hotel okay?*

I declined my sister's call and swiped away her texts. Without taking my meds or washing up, I scrambled out of bed and went straight for my laptop.

I could see my social media notifications from my cell, but I preferred the bigger screen.

And I needed to know if Valerie was alright this morning ...

Clearing away cans and empty chip bags, I rolled my computer chair up close to the screen.

The browser was still open on her page from where I'd left it last night. I refreshed, tapping my fingers noisily on the desk while I waited for it to load.

She's fine. Valerie Hutchens is always fine. And what does it matter if she's not, huh? She's not your sister; she's not your friend, not really. You barely know the fucking girl.

But I did know her, sort of. At least that's how it felt, as I followed her day-to-day movements, activities, and moods. As much as I hated to admit it, Valerie's mere existence was keeping me semi-sane while I hid, tucked away from the world in my shitty house, wasting away.

She seemed to be the only thing I could—or wanted—to focus on these days. And although our brief messages weren't much, she was the only living soul I'd communicated with—besides my sister and the doctors—since the accident.

I don't have any friends, no one I can talk to ... and although our short chats online probably meant nothing to her, they meant everything to me. Sure, I was jealous of her—her fragile beauty made me more self-aware of my own flaws, and her free-spirited travels and successful career highlighted my personal failures ... but Valerie was *hope*.

She was who I wanted to be ... a glimpse of who I might have been ...

My thoughts drifted over to the unopened Word files, which I couldn't see because Valerie's page was blocking the many icons that dotted the screen. Like Valerie, I was a writer. But not the kind that could ever get published. No, I'd stopped that kind of writing years ago. Now, I did some ghostwriting and occasionally, some freelance editing.

God knows I need the money. That's how I should be spending my time, not stalking people online.

I used to enjoy it, getting lost in other people's stories after I'd given up on my own ... but lately, all I wanted to do was stay up to date with Valerie's whereabouts and doings ... it was *her* story that intrigued me the most.

Frustrated, I clicked the refresh button again, and finally, Valerie's Instagram page filled my screen.

Nothing.

The last post was the live video I'd already watched. It had been posted at 2:06am.

I jumped up and ran back to my bedroom to retrieve my cell phone, then checked to make sure she hadn't posted any Snaps.

Nope—nothing.

By 4pm, I'd taken an hour-long "bath"—which involved me scrubbing myself with water and soap while I sat in my new shower chair that the doctor had recommended because it was too painful to get in and out of the tub if I sat all the way down inside it. I'd limped around my kitchen, sweeping the floor. I'd washed a sinkful of moldy dishes and started and stopped three editing projects that were due next month. As much as I wanted to stay busy and keep my mind from wandering back to Valerie, or something worse, I just couldn't focus. The words on the page were jumbly; my head throbbing; thick waves of red washing over my face and neck.

Valerie hadn't posted all day, nothing since that shaky, sinister live vid at 2 in the morning. I'd skimmed through nearly a thousand of her previous posts, and then her followers' posts ... I'd also sent her three direct messages, asking her how she was doing, if she was okay ... they had all gone unanswered.

Something is wrong. Something happened last night to Valerie.

I had gone so far as to make a scribbled list of hotels, motels, and inns that were in or around eastern Kentucky. There weren't many, and most of them were listed outside of Paducah. There was nothing in their local news either—no kidnappings, rapes, assaults ...

No murders.

I'm worried about a stranger; meanwhile, I can barely take care of myself. This is insane!

Once again, I pulled up a manuscript I'd been paid to edit. I made it through three lines, before my thoughts drifted back to her again and I couldn't read the words on the page. The shaky sound of Valerie's voice in that darkened street still haunted me ... she had seemed so afraid, so unsure of herself ...

I leapt from my computer chair as someone pounded on my front door.

I wasn't sure how to react. It had been so long since I'd had any visitors. My mind immediately thought of my neighbor, Karen. Or Carol, whatever her name was ... or possibly my physical therapist? But we didn't have an appointment and my neighbor had never stopped by before. I'd always assumed she was a hermit, like me, and that worked out well for both of us.

My heart thumping in my chest, I tiptoed over to the living-room window and peeked out through the dusty blinds.

"I see you, Camilla! Let me in!"

Fuck.

It was Hannah. Suddenly, it occurred to me that I hadn't answered any of my sister's texts today. Also, I hadn't taken my medicine. The switch-up in Valerie's routine was affecting my own.

Dammit.

Reluctantly, I unfastened the deadbolt and opened the door.

"Jesus. I was worried. I had to leave work an hour early ..." Hannah brushed past me, nearly knocking me over with her oversized purse and puffy pink coat.

Hannah was tall and elegant, with white-blonde hair. The polar opposite of me, with my short, chubby frame and dark-haired features. I'd often wondered if I was adopted.

You hatched from an egg, Milly. Fell out the back of a farmer's truck and went splat on the ground. You were lucky I scraped you up when I did. She had told me that when she was eight and I was four, and for some reason, the image had stuck with me.

My sister plopped down on my living-room sofa, dropped her purse by her feet, and kicked off a pair of shiny brown loafers.

"You alright?"

I was still guarding the door. I closed and locked it, breathing in through my mouth and out through my nose.

"I'm okay, Hannah. Just busy." Awkwardly, I sat down on the couch beside her.

She instantly launched into conversation, about how hectic her schedule was today—she'd been a dental hygienist since she was twenty, earning her associate's degree and completing her clinical practice in less than two years—and she reminded me, twice, that she'd had to take off early to come check on me.

Through all her chatter, her eyes never once met mine. *Even my own sister, my own blood, can't look at my ugly, disfigured face anymore.*

I wanted to reach over and shake her. Yell: *Bring my fucking sister back, please! She's the one I want. Not you. Not this bumbling girl who can't even look me in the face!*

And it's not just the *not*-looking that bothered me ... it's that every time I did leave the house—which wasn't often—people either quickly glanced away or stared straight at me, unapologetically, like I was some sort of circus freak ...

I missed the days of being looked at appreciatively by men and women; but mostly, I just missed being looked at like a normal person, another face in the crowd ...

"I'm sorry you came all this way. I promise, I'm fine. Just busy. I'm editing a manuscript for a client right now." *Maybe Hannah isn't the only one acting unlike herself. I, too, have been treating my sister like a stranger,* I realized, uncomfortably.

Hannah was staring across the room. I followed her gaze to my computer screen and the mess of cans and crud on the floor around my desk space.

The manuscript I was supposed to be working on was pulled up on the home screen (thankfully, I'd minimized Valerie's profile).

"I'm glad you're working and getting back in the swing of things. But what have you been doing for fun? You need to get out more. They miss you at the buffet."

The Pink Buffet was an old-timey restaurant that I'd worked at for nearly six years, before the accident. I'd used to go in early to set up prep for the buffet, and sometimes waitress in the evenings. I didn't miss it; and I didn't believe for a second that they missed me there either. The other girls were probably thrilled to have my extra hours.

I realized then that Hannah was still talking, although my mind was somewhere else. "Huh?"

"I was saying that we should do something together ... go catch a movie, or better yet, have one of those girls' nights at my place, where we stay up all night watching movies and ..."

"And drinking wine," I finished for her.

Wine. She can't even say it. Because she knows my drinking is what caused the accident in the first place.

Say it, Hannah. Look me in the face, for once, and say what you and everyone else is thinking: How could you be so reckless, Camilla?! How could you be a drunken fool, like Dad?

"What have you been doing for entertainment in this stuffy place?" Hannah pressed, breaking through my guilt-ridden thoughts.

What do I do for entertainment? I imagined myself telling her the truth: *I spend all day checking up on a girl I barely know, consumed by other people's lives while I watch my own shrivel up and disappear. How is that for fun, big sis?*

I opened my mouth, but nothing came out. I'd forgotten how to speak to her ... how to relate with anyone, for that matter.

How long has it been since I've spoken out loud to another person?

"I-I need to finish this. It's due tomorrow," I said hurriedly, pointing over at my screen. My couch was less of a couch, and more like a love seat, and the two squishy, smelly cushions were making me uncomfortable.

Too close. Hannah's sitting too close to me.

I stood up, suddenly, mindlessly rubbing the incision sites on my thighs.

"Thanks for checking up on me, though ..."

Hannah nodded, squeezing her lips together in a way that made me feel like she was disappointed in me.

You're not the only one, sis.

"Okay, I'll let you get back to what you were doing then," Hannah said, reluctantly rising from the couch. "Can I use your bathroom first? I've been holding it for hours."

"Sure. It's ..."

"I know where the bathroom is, Camilla." She gave me a strange look, her hazel eyes finally rising to meet mine. We stared each other down, a thick knot forming in my chest and throat.

We used to be so comfortable together, finishing each other's sentences, plucking thoughts straight from each other's brains and trying to guess what the other might say next ...

But those days are long gone. It's like we're strangers now. Don't cry, Camilla. Please don't cry ...

If you cry about missing your sister, then you'll cry about Chris. And if you cry about him ... well, you're liable to never stop. You'll die of dehydration from all those tears ...

It looked like I wasn't the only one fighting back tears. "Be right back," Hannah gulped, blinking rapidly as she turned down the short hallway.

I watched her disappear into the bathroom and moments later, I heard the water running. I paced back and forth in the living room, waiting for her to come back out. Minutes passed, and finally, I crept over to the computer. I bent down slightly, clicking the mouse to minimize the current document, before glancing over my shoulder to make sure Hannah was still in the bathroom. I could hear her opening and closing drawers—*is she snooping?*

I refreshed Valerie's page.

A new post!

Impulsively, I pulled my computer chair out and sat down, scooting in close to the screen.

My heartbeat echoed in my head as I quickly scanned the caption beneath the newly posted image. It was a sleepy-looking Valerie, nursing a cup of what looked like hot tea. Her hair was braided on one side, but carelessly loose, and she was wearing an oversized sweater that looked like something a grandma would knit.

What a long night and day … sorry guys, I hope you weren't worried. I have the worst stomach bug of my life, but I'm finally feeling better … going to nurse myself back to health because guess where I'm going tomorrow?! New Orleans! Look out Bourbon Street, here I come … #Nola #imnotfeelingwell #instasick

I breathed a sigh of relief. Why didn't it occur to me that she might simply be under the weather?

After all, perfect people get sick too.

She had responded to my messages, too! My eyes scanned quickly: **Thanks for asking. I'm fine, just a bit under the weather.** ☺

I stared at the smiley face, the corners of my own lips turning …

"Who's that?"

Startled to find Hannah standing behind me, I clumsily tried to close out the screen.

"Valerie, right?"

34

Too late.

I swallowed back the scream in my throat.

"Oh, yeah ... I remember her. You guys were in the same grade, weren't you?" Hannah was so close; I could feel her minty hot breath on the back of my neck. I shivered.

"Yeah, Valerie Hutchens. I don't really know her though. I was just scrolling through old classmates a few days ago and forgot to close out the screen." I shrugged, minimizing the page and spinning around and around in my computer chair.

Hannah clucked her tongue. "Yeah, wasn't she the one you were always jealous of? I never could understand what everybody saw in that girl. Especially you, Camilla."

I whipped around in my seat, turning so fast that my still-stiff neck from the accident roared with pain. "I wasn't jealous of her!"

But I could hear the defensive spike in my voice. "I wasn't," I mumbled.

I'm just lonely. And lost, I wanted to add. *And having someone to chat with, someone to pretend I'm friends with ... well, it helps a little. Maybe even a lot.*

"Okay, okay ... no offense. I think it would be good for you to reconnect with old friends, but ..."

"But what?" I thought about the sounds in the bathroom, her shuffling through my closet and drawers ...

"Are you taking your medication as prescribed?"

Ah, there it is. The real reason for her visit.

My eyes narrowed into tiny slits. "Of course I am. Why?"

35

Hannah held up her hands, defensively. "I'm just asking. Just worried about you, that's all … and you're not drinking, are you?"

"For fuck's sake, Hannah! No, I'm not drinking. What about you, huh? Still going out for Thirsty Thursdays with Mike?" I spat.

Hannah's face hardened and she didn't answer my question. Her eyes were traveling the room again … *She doesn't fucking believe me, does she?* I realized.

"Look, Hannah, I appreciate you coming by, but I need to get back to work. Time for you to go." I stood up and crossed my arms over my chest, waiting for her to take a hint and leave. "No offense."

Hannah frowned, her eyes zeroing in on mine once more. "I guess I'll see you later then," she huffed, scooping up her purse and seeing herself out.

From the window, I watched her climb into the driver's seat of her black Camry. Quietly, she sat, staring straight ahead at God knows what, for what felt like several minutes. Finally, she put the car in gear, and slowly reversed down the snaky driveway. I watched her taillights until they disappeared at the bottom of the hill.

Screw her! She was rude to me. It was her, not me, right?

Before I could waste any more time feeling guilty about my sister, I plopped back down in my desk chair and took a sip of flat Mountain Dew. Taking a deep breath, I clicked the refresh button on Valerie's page and reread her brief, but kind, message.

Chapter 3

I slept with my door closed and the ceiling fan on high, the spinning wood paddles lulling me to sleep ... *but now those paddles are the blades of a helicopter.*

A spotlight beams from overhead and the *whoosh, whoosh, whoosh* of the heavy blades signals that help is coming ...

"Don't worry. Help is on the way, Kid," Chris says, reading my mind.

Painfully, I twist my neck to the right, but then I remember ... *Chris is dead. I killed him ... oh, Chris ... it's all my fault, isn't it?*

I don't want to look ... don't want to see Chris that way again ... but he's talking.

He's talking! I just heard his voice!

I must have dreamed that he was dead ... he's still here ... he must be because he's talking, dammit!

But when I look at my husband, the parts of him that I love so much—his lips, his eyes, the dimple on his right cheek, the scar where his eyebrow piercing used to

37

be—those parts of him are gone. All that remains is a crumpled body in the passenger's seat. A body without a head. It doesn't even look real, like some sort of movie-set prop or clothing-store mannequin ...

And blood. *There's just so much of it ...*

"Back here, Kid."

Moaning, I force myself to lift one floppy arm and reach for the rearview mirror. It's slow and painful, like it's somebody else's arm—I'm commanding the arm to move, willing it with my mind like I'm telekinetic.

When the mirror is lowered, I can see the entirety of the backseat.

But where is his voice coming from ...?

Then everything comes into focus. In the rearview mirror, I come eye to eye with Chris.

Chris's head is in the backseat.

Chris's head is talking to me.

Chris: The Talking Head, is frowning.

"You promised. You promised me you'd stop drinking," his lips are moving.

"I know. I—I'm sorry ... I fucked up so bad ..."

"You lied. You're a liar ... you made me bleed ..."

A new voice breaks in.

"Ma'am, don't look back there. Look at me. Listen, you're in shock, but we're going to cut you out of there. There's a helicopter waiting to transport you to university hospital, okay? Keep your eyes on me and breathe."

The man is squatting down, looking in at me from

outside the shattered driver's window. His face smudgy and dark, my vision blurred ... but his voice is soothing and kind. I allow my eyes to lock onto his, sucking in huge gulps of air.

"Don't look at either of them. Look at me," comes a bell-like voice from my past. Slowly, painfully, I twist my neck to the right. Past the broken glass in the console, past the body that used to be Chris's in the passenger's seat ... there's a familiar face peering in at me through broken glass.

"Look at me, look at me ... focus only on me," says the girl with the bell-like voice.

The man is talking, Chris is talking, and somewhere inside my head I can hear them both pleading ... begging me not to look.

But it's not Chris's body in the passenger's seat that I'm looking at. It's the girl in the window. My gaze follows her wherever she goes ...

I can't peel my eyes away from her shining, beacon-shaped face. That smile, so contagious ...

Valerie.

I gave up on sleep hours ago.

This probably happened because I took my meds later than usual.

The dreams were always disruptive, but usually I slept at least six or seven hours before they caused me to shoot up out of bed, drenched in sweat and shaking.

My skin was still red with heat from the dream, a cool breeze shifting through the slope of trees that lined the back of my rental property. A cold chill rushed through my hair and blew it around my face.

I inhaled, closing my eyes as I tasted the wind.

I exhaled, tried to push the dream out of my mind. Tried to rid my body of memories and horrors that ran too deep ...

My iPhone sat on the flimsy lawn table beside me. I picked it up and held it to my chest.

You don't need it. It's a crutch. Promise me you'll stop drinking ... you don't act like yourself when you do, Chris's words whispered between the trees.

But I *did* need it—*a crutch.* Even before the accident, I'd struggled with anxiety my whole life. The alcohol dulled my nerves and created a sense of euphoria in a world where there was none for me. Even when I was happy, that pessimistic inner voice liked to spoil all my fun. Crutches helped. They allowed me to focus on something other than the deep dark voice inside me.

I never used to drink during the daytime—I had to work my food-prep job at The Pink Buffet. And after work, I'd either work extra hours, waiting tables, or I'd come home and write or edit until Chris came home. But in the evenings, after all the work was laid to rest ... I drank.

I drank until I promised Chris that I would stop.

Only, I didn't, not really ... I just got better at hiding it. I'd wait until he went to sleep at night, then I'd sneak sips into my soda water and fill my mouth with Listerine strips in between ... sometimes, drinking so late at night, that I was still half-drunk when I showed up for my early morning shift at the buffet.

My eyes still closed, I imagined sitting out on the back deck with Chris when we lived in our townhome. I could almost feel the squeeze of his hand on mine, his promise ring digging sharply into my palm ... *I'm proud of you for not drinking, Camilla. You're working hard to stay sober; I can tell.*

But it was all a farce ... *I was working hard to stay drunk, more like it.*

Liar ... his words from the dream rushed back at me.

Lies ... I told so many of them. *Even now, I can taste them—like vinegar on my tongue. They tasted bad, but they flowed like honey from my mouth ...*

Chris's hands—so tender and sweet—are squeezing harder and harder, choking the breath from my chest ...

Opening my eyes, I poked a finger at my phone, causing it to light up. I was surprised to find several unread texts from Hannah. She messaged me daily, but evening calls and texts were a rarity. Evenings were reserved for her and Mike.

Mike: the perfect husband. Mike: who was alive and still had a head. Mike: who went to bed early and woke up early. Who took my sister to dinner shows and vacations.

Things I never had a chance to do with Chris.

Hannah had sent several messages between 11pm and 12am, while I was dead asleep and dreaming.

41

Reluctantly, I opened them:

Hannah: I miss you, Milly.

Milly ... Hannah hadn't called me that in ages. Not since we were kids.

The endearing nickname made my throat and chest constrict, like peanut butter in my gullet.

Hannah: I'm sorry for the way I acted today. I just don't know what to say to you anymore. I don't know how to fix things the way I could when we were kids. You were young then, and you listened to me. Now ... now, I don't know how to help you. But I want to ... I want to help you, Milly.

Hannah: I'm sorry about what happened to you. I know you miss Chris. I miss him, too.

Hannah: But he's gone ... and now that Dad's gone too, all we have is each other.

Hannah: What I'm saying is ... I can't lose you.

Hannah: I love you, Milly. I miss you so much I can't breathe. Please come back to me.

When I closed my eyes this time, I was falling ... floating back to our farm house on Credence Drive. Hannah and I hiding in our bedroom closet ...

Don't move, she had whispered. *He's in the bedroom now.* I opened my mouth in horror, and like a little bird, a frightened chirp slipped out. Suddenly, her hands were wrapped around my face, covering my mouth and nose ... tight, so tight ... *I can't breathe!* The harder I fought, the firmer her clamp became. I tried to scream

42

but couldn't. *Shhh ... just a few more minutes,* she had promised.

My mother died of cancer before I was old enough to know her. My father coped with her loss by drinking. And he wasn't a funny drunk or a clumsy drunk ... he was mean. Hannah and I would hide in the closet, or wherever we could, until he finished one of his rampages.

There's not a horror movie in the world that could make my heart race the way Dad could ...

I shook that memory away and opened my eyes. My phone chimed again. A notification this time: Valerie had made a new post!

I lit another cigarette, pushing aside thoughts of my sister, ignoring the sharp burn in my chest, and opened my Instagram app.

I was disappointed to find that she hadn't posted a new video or picture of herself. It was simply a faded blue image with a quote, like the bored-as-fuck ones I saw on my Facebook feed daily.

My eyes scanned the words ... they were familiar, but where had I seen them before—a book, or a movie, maybe? I typed the first sentence of the quote into Google and instantly, results for that old Beatles song, *Eleanor Rigby*, popped up.

It was a song about lonely people, like me. A woman who died in a church, all alone. For the life of me, I couldn't remember the rest of the song, beyond the first verse.

Pulling up YouTube, I found the song within seconds and clicked play.

Before I could change my mind, I was typing out another message to Valerie.

Me: I haven't heard this song in years. It's so haunting, so beautiful … hope you're feeling better today.

Usually, it took Valerie hours—sometimes, days—to respond. But she immediately wrote back, sending a slither of pleasure right through me.

Valerie: Me too. It always helps me sleep.

Eyes closed, I leaned my head back in the lawn chair, letting that haunting old song consume me, all the while imagining Valerie, sick and alone in her hotel room a few hundred miles away, doing the exact same thing.

Paul McCartney's timeless voice … *was it Paul or John, John or Paul …?* No matter—their words lulled me back to sleep like a pill …

The next day, my face was sporting a sun burn—I'd made the mistake of falling asleep out on the back porch, and I'd slept through the early morning sunrise and into the afternoon.

The red, raw shine to my cheeks made me feel almost normal—it had been a long time since I'd felt the sun, since my face had a sheen of color to it. Hannah and I had used to go to the beach every summer with our dad … oh, how we blistered in the sun while he got hammered at the beach bar all day. For some reason, we enjoyed the habit of peeling burnt skin off each other's shoulders and noses.

I finished a bowl of Fruity Pebbles and drank a glass

of orange juice, thoughts funneling back to my sister's late-night texts ...

I need to call her today. Set things straight with her once and for all.

Because she was right—she *was* all I had left in this world. I needed to focus on her, and getting my life back in order, not chasing old ghosts from high school ... not reliving that horrendous night with Chris. It was lonely here—and like that girl in the church all alone, I didn't want to die in this apartment. *If I did, how long would it take for someone to find me ... days, weeks, months? Hannah probably won't be back for a while, after how I treated her yesterday ...*

But some habits die hard—by one o'clock, I found myself back in my usual computer chair, eagerly scoping out Valerie's page for updates. I wanted to send more messages, but I refrained. I couldn't make myself look *too* desperate.

I'd missed a video she'd posted at 4am. While I was sleeping to the tune of *Eleanor Rigby*, Valerie had made another update. I clicked on her video, trying to force myself not to care ...

Like me, Valerie was sitting at a desk. Albeit, a clean one. It looked generic with nothing on its surface; she was obviously still in her hotel room. Behind her, I could see the silhouette of a queen-sized bed in the dark. Blankets and sheets crumpled up like blobby white ghosts.

Billowy white curtains blew behind her, too ... the room

was dark, shadows dancing across the walls ... Valerie's face, pale and ghoulish, stared back at me through the screen.

She must still be feeling sick.

Her expression was grim, a tightness to her cheeks and eyes I'd never seen before. I'd never seen her look so ... *unfiltered.*

"I don't know if it's this stomach bug, or what ... I could be losing my mind. I went out for dinner and a movie by myself tonight, and once again, I couldn't shake the feeling that I was being followed. I don't talk much about my personal life here, but mental illness does run in my family ... anyways, pray for me, will ya? I mean, if that's your thing ... okay? I have a flight to catch in the morning and I need to get my head on straight before I head out."

A shadow shifted in the room behind her, giving my stomach a jolt. There was something moving behind the curtains in the background!

What the hell is that?

Valerie kept on talking, oblivious, but I could no longer hear the words ... my eyes were glued to the spot where the shadow had been.

She'd left the window open ...

"I'll check in tomorrow once I land in Louisiana. Good night, world."

And just like that, the shadow moved. For a brief second, I caught a clear glimpse of a man's face peeking out from between the curtains. My heart fluttered in my chest. He was looking through her hotel window!

"Behind you ..." I breathed, a chill running from the top of my scalp down to my toes. But then the video came to an end. I stared at the blank, dark screen, a rattle of fear in my bones.

The video wasn't live. She posted this eight hours ago, I realized in horror.

And a quick scan through her pages revealed that she hadn't posted anything else since.

Did I really see what I thought I saw, or am I losing my mind just like Valerie thought she was losing hers?

I re-played the video again and again, slowing it down as much as I possibly could. There was no doubt in my mind—a man was looking in at Valerie while she had her back turned to the window. It was too clear not to be real. Not a trick of the shadows ... or my mind, for that matter.

And although his face was dark and a little fuzzy, there was something familiar about it too ...

The man in the window looks like Chris.

A knock of fear jerked me out of my seat. I stood up, pacing back and forth in front of the computer. This wasn't the first time I'd seen the Chris-lookalike either. *It's impossible—I know it's not Chris. But damn, he does look a whole lot like him. It's unsettling.*

I'd noticed him in another one of Valerie's posts ... *but which one?*

The reason the man stood out to me the first time was because he *did* sort of look like Chris, although, rationally, I knew it wasn't him.

I sat back down, clicking through her old photos and posts ... *thousands and thousands of photos! Too many ...*

But then, a few minutes later, I found exactly what I'd been looking for ...

There!

It was an old post, from before I'd started following her every move ... but I'd scrolled through these old photos so many times ...

There.

He was standing two rows behind her at an outdoor concert in Ohio. Valerie was smiling, extending the camera with one hand and holding up the other to show a bracelet—a backstage VIP band circling her wrist. It was a hodge-podge of alternative bands, but she'd specifically referenced a Marilyn Manson song in her caption: *#RockisDead*.

The reason the man had caught my attention the first time, besides the fact that he kind of looked like Chris, was because he was staring so intensely into the camera from several rows back, almost like he'd accidentally looked at the wrong moment and gotten captured in Valerie's photo forever ... *a classic photo-bomb.* Annoying, but not uncommon. All the smudgy little faces in the background of her videos and pictures ... *unassuming strangers, or are they?*

I just assumed it was an accident, an odd guy looking in the background, his serious spot-on gaze captured by the lens ...

And there! Another pic in Florida—he looked like any

other guy you'd see ... just a man having a drink at a tiki bar, enjoying his vacation while some girl—*Valerie*—snapped a selfie of her bikini-clad self, holding a sugary-rimmed margarita. It was a sideview of his face at the bar ... *it might not be him.*

But it sure as hell looked like him. And I couldn't shake the eerie realization that he looked so similar to Chris ... the slope of his jaw, that slightly off-center nose ... even the blue-black, closely cropped hair was the same.

Valerie was the kind of girl that was prone to admirers. *But that face in the window ... that went way beyond normal obsession.*

Valerie had a stalker besides me. A real one.

What if she's in serious danger?

49

Chapter 4

It was warm for October, the wind whispering through the trees behind my apartment, circulating stuffy puffs of air through the open window above my bed. The sill was covered in dust, the window practically jammed shut as I'd fought to wrench it open ... it'd been so long since I'd opened a window. *Since I'd let the world inside.*

But I needed the extra air. My room was too itchy, too tight. And I couldn't shake off my concerns ... *What I really can't shake off is Valerie Hutchens.*

After I'd spotted the mystery man in Valerie's video, I'd called the cops, jumped in my dad's old Chevy truck, and raced all the way to Kentucky to save her ... *no. No, I didn't.*

But what I did do was play out all these fantasy, next-move scenarios. They rolled through my head in waves, playing out like a black-and-white, made-for-TV movie, reverberating in my ears. *Shouldawouldacoulda ... what should I do?!*

Every scenario had the same outcome ... me: the hero. Valerie: the damsel in distress. Cue credits ...

But the truth was, Valerie hadn't posted anything in two days. Nothing at all since the creepy video with the Chris lookalike in the background. She hadn't gone two days, or even one day, without posting in months. Not until recently.

I'd carried my laptop from the living room to my bedroom, so I could sulk under the covers and wonder what she was up to ...

I couldn't help thinking about that video she'd posted the night before I saw the man ... about a stalker following her home, and that speech about needing a hero. *Valerie knew she was in danger, so why didn't she call the cops?*

No stupid quotes, no videos, no pics ... no responses to my messages either.

I'd scanned the comments beneath the latest video, quietly hoping and wishing that one of her many followers would also spot the man in the window.

No one had. Not even her oldest admirer, Luke, had noticed. He'd liked the video and moved on, just like everyone else. I waited for comments that mentioned the man, but there were none. But they did offer her well wishes and platitudes ...

Her followers told her not to worry. They wished her well on her trip to New Orleans. They told her to 'get better soon'. They threw around 'prayers' like handfuls of confetti.

They said all the stupid things that people say when they know there's nothing else to be said.

But how did no one else see the man?

The fact that he looked like Chris was fucking with me ... *Could it all be in my own head? Am I losing my mind, just as Valerie thought she was losing hers ...?*

No. The photos from her old posts proved it—this wasn't the man's first, or even second, encounter with Valerie. He was obviously following her—*stalking her*—and closely enough to be captured in the background on three occasions now. *How many more times had he been around, only he didn't get captured in a photo?* I wondered. *And he's not Chris. Just because he has dark eyes and hair, and a similar build, doesn't make him Chris ...*

Chris is dead.

Hannah had texted me today, like clockwork:

Hannah: I tried to call again. Can we chat on the phone? You never responded to my messages the other day. You okay?

My imaginary response: *No ... no, I'm not okay. I'm worried about a woman I barely know. Unable to help her because I can't leave my apartment—correction: won't leave my apartment. And even if I did—if I could—what the hell good would it do? A man that looks like my dead husband is following a girl I haven't seen in over a decade ... and for some reason, I'm bent out of shape about it.*

I didn't know Valerie's exact location. I didn't know who the man in the window was, or if Valerie was in some sort of danger ...

I rotated my thumbs, hesitating, before finally, I typed back to Hannah:

Me: Doing well! Working hard on a writing project. Talk soon, I promise.

Working hard, indeed.

In reality, I was working hard not to fall apart because my latest addiction had run dry.

Oh, Valerie. I need my fix.

Her un-updated page stared back at me like an empty syringe.

Or an empty glass.

I clicked send, then added another message to my sister:

Me: Miss you too, Hannah. I'm fine. Really.

What am I going to do if Valerie never comes back online? I wondered. I had to do something to help her ... to check up on her ... *but what if something terrible has already happened? What if I'm too late?*

My thoughts were quickly spinning out of control. I could ask Hannah for advice, tell her what was going on ... but then she'd just give me that look, the one from the other day ... that look of disapproval and concern. *She thinks I'm a drunk and a pill addict ...*

I sat up in bed and refreshed my browser. For the hundredth time today, I checked local crime reports in Kentucky. I checked Indiana and Ohio, too, since they were close. Lastly, I checked New Orleans. *Nada.*

There were crimes, plenty of them. Burglary, assault, driving while intoxicated ... but no mention of a young pharmaceutical rep vanishing from her hotel room. No pretty-girl murders splashed dramatically across the front

53

page, no catchy taglines about stalkers or kidnappings ...

As popular as Valerie was online, I wasn't sure how long it would be before her real-life friends or family missed her. She had an aunt who lived in town ... Janet, she said her name was. But Valerie's employer ... surely, *they* would know if she never made it to New Orleans. *Wouldn't they?*

I rolled onto my back, staring up at the popcorn patterns on the ceiling above my bed. They swirled, triggering a sick rush of something in my gut ... *fear? No, not fear—memory.* I blinked slowly, the tilt-o-whirl roof from the night of the accident flashing like a blinking bulb in my face. *Chris's voice, pleading in the dark ... was he pleading or screaming ...?*

Fuck. I have to do something. I can't just sit here and do nothing to help her.

Valerie worked for a company called Rook Pharmaceuticals. They weren't the biggest branch of big pharma, but they were damn near close.

For one silent second, my next move became clear.

Valerie could be in danger. And if there's no one to help her or warn her, then I could be the only one who does.

As I sat up, there was a new form of energy pumping through my veins.

I composed my message in a Word document, then read over it a dozen times before finally copying and pasting it into a message on Instagram. I exhaled, then clicked send:

Valerie,

I know it's none of my business, but I couldn't help

but notice something strange in the background of your latest video. A strange man peering in the window behind you. I noticed him in the background of some of your other pictures as well. I know we don't know each other well and we weren't all that close in school ... but I'm worried about you. After that other video about the man following you from the bar, I was a little concerned that maybe the man in the window was him ... that maybe you have a stalker. Please write me back.

Next, I looked up the phone number for Rook Pharmaceuticals. The receptionist who answered was young, her words breathy and practiced.

My words, on the other hand, sounded like someone else's—throaty and strained.

I cleared my throat, "My name is Janet Hutchens. My niece is employed as a rep with your company."

Silence.

"Umm ... her name is Valerie. She was traveling on business to Kentucky, and then her next stop was New Orleans. I've been unable to reach her on her cell the last couple days, and I was hoping you had another line where I could reach her. Or could you just check in on her, please?"

"Yes. Just a moment." The "Yes" part gave me cause for hope, but still, I had a bad feeling that giving out info about their young, attractive, female reps was against company policy. *If not, it probably should be.*

Papers shuffled in the background and I could hear the receptionist striking keys.

"We have a lot of reps on staff, ma'am. I'll write down her name and see what I can find out. May I call you back?"

Shit. Call me back?

The thought of leaving my number, a number that could easily get funneled back to Valerie somehow, shook me to the core. *No, no I can't leave my number. It's one thing to send a concerned message on social media, it's another to call her work pretending to be a worried family member. She'll think I'm insane if she finds out I called Rook, impersonating Janet.*

My heart was throbbing in my ear drums. "Uh ... I'm sorry. I'm having trouble hearing you. Please check on my niece. I'll call back in about an hour."

Clicking end before the chirpy receptionist could respond, I fell back on the bed, breathless.

It was hard to believe that doing normal things—like sending a message or having a phone conversation with another human being—could cause this much anxiety.

I held my hand to my chest, sucking in deep, craggy breaths.

There's no way Valerie will find out it was me. It could have been anyone calling ...

I didn't plan on calling back. I'd done my part. I couldn't take the chance of Valerie finding out about her weird former classmate checking up on her at work. By the look of things, Valerie had enough admirers without adding me to the list ...

At least now, though, maybe someone will check in on her and make sure she's doing okay. Won't they?

Slightly satisfied, I refreshed Valerie's Instagram page. *Still nothing.*

Please be okay, Valerie, I secretly wished. I wasn't sure if she would write back or not, but I felt strangely giddy about the fact that I'd written her a heartfelt message. I wasn't just her follower; I was her friend—and I needed to know that she was okay.

There was a can of flat Sprite on my bedside table. Cupping the can, I took a slow sip, remembering how good Sprite used to taste in a white-wine spritzer. Especially when I chased it with a few shots of something stronger ...

I added my night-time pills to my dinner plate, which consisted of waffles from a box in the freezer and slimy, out-of-date syrup.

For once, I was using the kitchen table. A dinette really, with only two chairs and enough room to clank two plates together. Chris would have liked it—he was a minimalist, or he used to be, always getting mad at me for buying clunky furniture and too many pans. It wasn't the stuff I enjoyed buying, it was the shopping itself, buying things just for us and our little, two-person family. It made me feel domesticated and happy. Although, I'm not sure Chris would have agreed ...

It had been hours since I'd sent the message and made the call to Valerie's employer, the day floating by with heady longing ... longing for something ... I couldn't put my finger on.

57

My phone blipped, startling me in the silent kitchen. I picked it up, pushing my chair back with a screech as I read the words: **_TheWorldIsMine_26 started a live video. Watch it before it ends!**

Yes!

My hands were shaking with adrenaline. Instead of getting up and going to my laptop, I clicked on the video from my phone.

The screen was dark.

Maybe she's waiting, giving everyone a chance to get online …

I turned the volume on my phone all the way up, holding my breath. Listening.

At first, I couldn't see or hear anything. Just static. Groaning, I walked over and flipped out all the lights in the kitchen. I tried to zero in on the pitch-black screen.

In the dark, I watched and waited. *But what am I waiting for?*

"Where are you, Valerie?" I whispered.

The screen was still dark, but now I could almost hear … muffled voices, a man and a woman talking …

"I don't have it. I never did. You can't do this. Someone will come …" said the woman, her voice barely above a whisper. *Was it Valerie's voice?* I strained to hear more, no longer looking at the video, but pressing my ear up to the screen.

"Please."

Please. It was one simple word, barely audible, but I had no doubt: it was Valerie talking.

The video cut off, the comments below filling up with silly emojis and 'Where ya at?'s and 'Oopsie's.

I watched the comments coming in, refreshing often, a sense of dread bubbling over inside me.

Finally, a new comment appeared, this one different from the rest. This one had an edge of concern to it.

'Valerie, call me now. I can't reach you.'

It was from a follower I hadn't noticed before ... not a frequent poster, apparently. I clicked on her face and pulled up her profile: **Janet Haukemeyer.**

I'd never seen this woman before, even though I'd pretended to be her hours earlier. But I instantly knew who she was: Valerie's aunt. Looking at her picture gave me a strange feeling, like I was looking at another version of Valerie, only it was forty years into the future.

So, this is Aunt Janet.

Suddenly, it was like someone else was taking over my body—in a frenzy, I started clicking, searching every social media site I could online. Anything that contained the words 'Janet Haukemeyer' and 'Oshkosh, Wisconsin'.

Immediately, I got a hit. Janet Haukemeyer was a painter, and like most normal people online, she had a Facebook profile, Twitter page, and LinkedIn account. She also had an Instagram page but hadn't posted anything new in two years. I scanned through her pictures—mostly paintings, some photography. No pictures of her and Valerie. Her Facebook page was locked down, too, privacy settings set to "Fort Knox" or whatever the most private of settings were ...

Damn. No help.

I waited for Aunt Janet to leave more comments. For anyone else to start worrying besides me ...

Impulsively, I sent another message to Valerie:

Me: Valerie, please let me know that you're okay! Are you in trouble? Can I help?

And then it happened—a tiny ding on my cell phone. *Valerie responded to my message!*

Shell-shocked, I slunk back down in my chair at the table and read her message again and again. It was short; only two lines:

I don't know who to turn to. I don't know who can help ...

Feverishly, I typed back:

Are you in danger? Want me to call the police?

Her response was instantaneous:

NO.

I leaned back in my chair, unsure how to respond. Finally, I typed:

Valerie, tell me what's going on.

I stared at the phone for what felt like hours, minutes painfully ticking by.

I can't write about it on here. Can you come to Paducah? PLEASE. I NEED A FRIEND.

Chapter 5

*P**lease. I need a friend.*

Valerie needed my help, but why?

I'd sent a dozen follow-up messages: **Where are you?**
Why don't I just call the cops? I'll need directions if you
want me to come ...

My body buzzed with adrenaline as I floated around my
room, tossing shirts and panties into a duffel bag I hadn't
used in years ... *Can I really do this? This is nuts!*

Finally, with my bag bulging with clothes and toiletries,
I sat on the scruffy carpet, clutching the bag to my chest
like a shield.

Valerie still hadn't written me back. *She can't really want*
me to come there ... can she?

Valerie Hutchens—with her million-dollar smile and her
ten thousand followers ... why does she need *me* to come?

But then my mind drifted back to the comments on her
page ... her followers, with their cookie-cutter responses ...
not a single one of them had noticed the man. But *I* had.

I'd reached out to her, and now, she was reaching back.

Valerie needs me. Maybe she's not writing back because she's in danger.

I got up, slowly, and went to the bathroom. Under the glaring lights, I smeared thick, cakey concealer on my face—it did nothing to help my scars—then I lifted the hood of my sweatshirt over my head, a lame attempt at concealing my face.

There are few things that could motivate me to leave this house—but Valerie … maybe this is my chance.

Valerie was my only friend. Maybe I was her only real friend, too.

Anxiety ran through me like an electric current. With my keys in one hand and my bag in the other, I took a few steps toward the door.

Wait. I need something. A little extra courage …

I returned to the bathroom.

Hannah was right about one thing, one thing she hadn't forgotten … the bathroom had always been my favorite hiding place.

But sometimes, you have to go the extra mile to hide things from yourself …

In the top of my closet, I reached for a slimy old jar of petroleum jelly. It's one of those items that everyone has, but rarely uses … well, I had a use for mine.

Screwing off the lid, I dipped my fingers inside the still-sticky, scraped-out jar. My fingers closed around a shot-sized bottle of vodka.

Parking at the curb on Apple Drive, I found myself five doors down from my sister's house. My chest burned, my head swimming in a way I hadn't felt in months ...

It had been so long since I'd gone outside, beyond my porch. Since I'd smelled the air in the town of Oshkosh ... since I'd tasted the courage that comes from alcohol.

The drive to my sister's house had felt like an out-of-body experience. I'd had tunnel vision for most of the drive, but now that the vodka had settled in, I was feeling better.

I'm outside. I did it! Valerie not only wants my help, she needs it ...

The air smelled sweeter, sharper than I remembered ... I could almost taste somebody's leftover supper in the air. As I followed the sidewalk to my sister's house, my footsteps echoing on the quiet street, I caught a whiff of used diapers.

Apple Lane. Is it possible for a street to look happy?

If so, Apple Lane was a pure delight.

I stopped outside my sister's dining-room window, in awe of the life she'd made for herself. The house was brick, two-story. Two perfectly shaped pumpkins dotted each side of the grand entranceway.

Mike and Hannah had no children. *Did they sit and carve these pumpkins together?*

I could picture Hannah, in my mind's eye, penciling in 'Carve pumpkins with Mike' on her monthly calendar.

They were grinning, the slimy pegs of pumpkin teeth perfectly aligned and evenly spaced. I shivered.

When we were little, Hannah and I didn't carve pump-kins. But we did chuck some of the neighbors' pumpkins at people's houses. The kids who had perfect families and perfect pumpkins … even though we never said so, they were always our targets.

I missed those times with Hannah. Times when there was no Mike, no Chris … no dead husbands chasing me in my dreams …

My sister had traded in childish shenanigans for cardi-gans and six o'clock dinners and husbands who don't yell when they're mad. Husbands who don't wrap their hands around your throat when you've pissed them off …

Now that I was here, I felt foolish for coming.

I'd come to tell her about Valerie. I'd come to ask her to either stop me, or come with me … which one, I wasn't sure.

Anchored to the ground outside their window, I watched Hannah and Mike from where I stood. They were seated across from each other at the dining-room table. The curtains were wide open, the fancy chandelier above the table creating a prism of sparkling diamond shapes around the room.

Beneath my feet, the grass felt squishy and soft … I imagined it were like quicksand, slowly pulling me under as I watched my sister's happy, smiling face.

Pass the bread please, I imagined Hannah saying as Mike, with his Rolex watch and dorky, plaid pullover, handed her a plate of what looked like garlic sticks.

The window was closed, but I swear I could smell the soft buttery bread … taste a smidge of salt on my tongue.

Mike said something as he passed the bread. Possibly, probably: *Sure thing, dear.*

Like a ghost, I remained there, unseen. After several minutes, I turned and walked back to the truck.

Tears blurred my eyes as I rolled through the stop sign and pulled away from Sunny Springs subdivision.

My sister's life on Apple Lane is sunny and perfect, and the last thing she needs is me showing up at her door, begging her to go on a road trip with me.

Two miles down the road, I whipped my truck to the side and took out my phone. I checked both Valerie's and Janet's pages for updates, I checked for a new message—nothing. I felt an ache in my stomach I'd never felt before ... a need to do something, but unsure what exactly.

There were a few thousand dollars in my bank account. More than I used to have, when I lived check-to-check working at the buffet. But since the accident, I hadn't been working. Instead, I'd been living off a small inheritance I'd gotten from my dad when he died. *A few g's doesn't feel like much when you're not working and have no plans to return.* It would all be gone in a few months, tops, what with the cost of my rent, utilities, toiletries, and groceries.

No money coming in, a decent amount going out each month ... dwindling away like dust in a windstorm.

I could have sold my dad's truck for a few thousand dollars, but it was the only thing of his that I still owned.

Hannah had taken most of the small things, but I had the truck ... I couldn't sell it.

I'm like a ship that is full of holes, sinking faster by the minute. And it's not like I don't know how to swim, how to get my head above water ... it's just that I don't want to.

I had nothing to lose anymore, except for Valerie. She was my one pastime ... and now she was in trouble. I had to help her.

Oshkosh resembled a ghost town as I made a slow left onto Main Street. The six o'clock dinner hush clung to the air as I rolled up to a stop light.

Is everyone sitting around their tables, passing bread to one another? Am I the only one alone in this town?

So much had changed since the last time I was here ... but then again, nothing had changed at all.

Residential buildings lined each side of the street, like graves, dark and devoid of life.

The sign for *Roberta's* hardware shop was old and fading, but it gleamed, the *s* flickering off and on, and making the head pain return.

There wasn't a soul in sight.

But then karma intervened, as she often does, and from the corner of my eye, I spotted movement on the sidewalk. An old lady emerged from the store, tugging on a newly purchased Black & Decker. *Well, I'll be damned.*

The light melted back to green, but my foot was stuck on the brake pedal. *Paralyzed.*

The old lady turned her head and our eyes met.

I can just imagine how I must look right now … hair twisted into a sloppy bun, ghost-white makeup on my face. *My face!*

I'd nearly forgotten my scars. I held up a hand, trying to cover them.

But the lady was smiling—*smirking, really*—and I knew she had seen me.

Because Bonnie Brown sees everything.

Bonnie had every reason to smirk at my scars, every reason in the world to hate me … after all, it was I who caused the death of her son.

But my ex-mother-in-law had hated me long before I killed him. Oh, how the Browns loathed "outsiders". On family holidays, I'd kept my mouth shut and sat at the table with all the other "others"—Chris's brother's wife, his cousin's girlfriend-of-the-month …

I haven't seen Bonnie since the accident.

Bonnie gripped the vacuum handle with one hand. Slowly, she lifted the other. For one brief, hopeful moment, I thought she was going to wave at me. But then she pointed. It was only then that I heard the sound, a blaring car horn behind me. In the rearview mirror, a teenage boy in a black Volvo shook his arms wildly back and forth. And beside me, Bonnie was still staring, only she wasn't smiling anymore. I opened my mouth. Waited for the scream to come.

But it didn't … *it never does* …

I smashed my foot down on the gas pedal, the truck jolting forward dangerously. As I self-corrected and straightened up the wheel, I glanced back in the mirror. I couldn't see my mother-in-law anymore. But the boy behind me was angry; he swerved into the lane beside me, lips silently moving—cursing me, no doubt. He passed me on the right.

"Sorry," I mumbled, watching his taillights disappear down the street.

Sorry. I smacked both hands on the steering wheel.

Sorry. Sorry. Sorry.

Jesus, I'm fucking sorry.

A thousand times I'd said that word—*sorry*—after the accident ... to Chris's family, to my sister, to strangers ... to a version of Chris that didn't exist anymore, to a phantom in the sky.

But my apologies made no difference. And nothing made a difference when it came to the Browns. They hadn't even let me attend my own husband's funeral.

He was cremated. His body and soul reduced to gravel and bits.

They'd suggested that I have my own separate ceremony for Chris. Only "family and friends" were allowed to attend theirs ... and of course I didn't fit *that* bill.

The Browns knew good and well that my mother and father were dead, that the only living relative I had left was my sister.

I could hear them now, the whispers at the funeral:

Camilla had her own ceremony for Chris.

I heard the whole family showed up: party of two.

Cue laughter.

I didn't ease up on the gas until the main strip of town melted like butter from my periphery.

I drifted past cornfields and farmhouses until there was nothing but trees and pastures. Branches swayed on both sides of me, their bony fingers reaching down for the truck, their whispers floating through the open cracks in my windows ...

Through the blurry trees that whizzed by, I could make out a set of twinkling lights. *The water tower.* It was there that Chris had proposed.

We'd carried bottles of beer to the top, climbing slowly, and nervously, up the rickety, twisted stairs.

The top of the tower opened into a small, empty room. From all sides you could see the entire town of Oshkosh. The view was breathtaking, but my eyes were drawn to Chris.

That cramped space at the top of the tower was barely large enough for the two of us ... but we kept scooting closer, passing a bottle of beer back and forth. And finally, long after midnight, we were properly drunk enough to make out. Like teenagers, we were hungry with lust, ravenous and breathy as we kissed and petted ... eventually, Chris laid flat on his back, and although it was uncomfortable as hell, he pretended it wasn't, and he offered his chest as a pillow for me.

It was a few months later that he took me back there to propose.

The water tower was one spot, but there were so many more. There were traces of Chris all over town. The one-stop-shop where we picked up milk and a carton of eggs on Saturdays. The donut shop we frequented on special occasions. The church where we were married.

Inside my drab prison cell, I was safe from reminders. But here ... *here*, I couldn't avoid Chris's ghost for long. *He is everywhere.*

Despite seeing Bonnie and places that reminded me of Chris, it did feel good to drive. I rolled the driver's window all the way down, letting the October chill rush in; suddenly, it felt easier to breathe than it had in months ... more air to go around out here in the open, not dense like the air in my tomb-like apartment.

The outside world is a scary place, but so is being isolated ... inside, outside ... does it really make a difference? My life is miserable either way ... but Valerie ... maybe now I'll have a chance to do something different. A road not traveled before ...

Suddenly, the trees evaporated and the neighboring town of Mirasu emerged. The lights on the hamburger stand and ice-cream parlor blinked back at me, accusatory: *red black red black red black.*

Can't we stop? I'm starving, Chris had said.

The fair has better food, Chris. You promised me a Snickers, remember? You even said you'd try one. They're not gross, I promise ...

There was a syrupy tone in my voice, my tongue thick

70

and dry the way it always was when I'd had too much to drink.

But Chris hadn't noticed ... *How could he not know I'd been drinking? Why was he no longer paying attention?*

The tiny mom-and-pop eateries swished past as I sped up. The site of the crash was coming, only a few miles ahead ... I hadn't come this way since, since ... I hadn't been this way at all since the accident, I realized.

Okay, have it your way. You always do. Chris squeezed my leg, his fingers trailing up and under the hem of my skirt ...

His fingers were rough—too rough. *Fucking stop!* I'd screamed.

Signs for the highway emerged.

I flipped my right blinker on, but instead of taking the highway, I yanked my wheel hard to the left.

If you blinked, you'd miss the skinny dirt road that led up Hogman's Hill. I skidded, then self-corrected, and slowed down to a crawl.

I needed to make a quick stop at my mother-in-law's house.

Chapter 6

Bonnie Brown's two-bedroom house was perched at the pinnacle of the hill, looking down on me. If there were neighbors, they were deep down the sides of the hill, out of sight.

The small bungalow was picturesque, flower baskets dangling from the awnings in the front. They creaked in the wind, swinging back and forth, like a warning.

Each window was dark, encased in pale-blue shutters, and a slow curl of smoke arose from the chimney. I knew that no one was home, but I couldn't shake the eerie feeling of being watched as I slowly wrenched open the door to the truck.

Bonnie's house had always reminded me of that gingerbread house in Hansel and Gretel. Cutesy. Homey. *Evil lurking inside it.*

But my ex-mother-in-law wasn't evil, not really. She was unkind to outsiders, and overly protective of her children—not a criminal trait, just an annoying one.

I didn't know exactly how she'd react to my presence

here, but one thing was certain: I wouldn't be welcome. *Would she claw my eyes out, vengeance for her beloved son? Or would she simply turn me away?* For my sake, I hoped to never find out.

Her Subaru was nowhere in sight. I slammed the door to the truck and ticked the minutes off on my fingers, trying to calculate her possible distance. She would have had to load up that vacuum and then drive home, and Bonnie always drove the speed limit. *Also, who's to say she didn't have more errands to run?* For my sake, I prayed that she had several.

I wasn't here to confront her or hide in the bushes and spring-attack when she got back. No ... I'd come here for one reason, and one reason only: *to take what is mine.*

The urn belongs with me, not her.

I'd imagined this moment so many times in my fanta-sies ... taking my revenge, stealing my husband's urn. And seeing her on Main Street, it made me realize that it was now or never. *Who knows how long it will be before I leave the house again? Might as well make the most of it before I hit the road to find Valerie ...*

In the back of the house, Chris's old Dodge was parked somewhere ... but I refused to go around and look. Too many memories of us riding together, me scurrying to the middle seat to get closer to him ...

I still carried Chris's old keyring, and it rattled in my hand, the jingle an ominous sound on the too-quiet, windy hillside. On it were keys to my apartment, the truck, Chris's truck, and keys to the now-totaled Buick. I shivered in the dark, wind whistling through my hair, which was greasy and damp with sweat.

I'm about to break into someone's house. This must be a new low for me. But then I imagined Chris's body, slumped and headless, bloodied in the seat beside me ... *No, this is a minor blip in my history of misdoings.*

The keyring also held a spare key to Chris's mother's house.

The front porch light was on as I plunged the key into the lock and turned it. It clicked, and as the front door creaked open, I took in a sharp breath.

I should have been afraid.

I should have turned around.

Should have jumped back in the truck and gone home ...

If I stopped to think about what I was doing for one second, my rational side would take over ... *but that part of me is fading ...*

Too late to turn back now.

Keep on going.

If Bonnie caught me sneaking inside her house ... at best, she'd call the cops. At worst, she'd blow a jagged hole through my head with the 9mm handgun Chris bought her two Christmases ago.

Fuck it. Now or never, remember?

I nudged the door with my black combat boot. Then, feeling confident that no one was inside, I prodded it the rest of the way open.

Bonnie had been a widow for as long as I'd known Chris; all her kids were grown. Well, most of her kids were ... *one of them is dead because of you,* I reminded myself, grimly.

"Anybody home?" my voice was a shrill squeak in the silent darkness.

Rich smells of cooking oil, flour, and ginger permeated the air.

As I looked around the kitchen, with its old-timey apple and duck designs, the holidays spent here with Chris came rushing back to me. My stomach filled with a sour sense of dread. No, not dread ... *remorse. A flash of a former life ... a former version of me that was semi-happy.*

I was happy, wasn't I? Sure, his family didn't like me much. But Chris ... his love had been fiery, and doggedly loyal.

I just need to get in and out, quickly. Get this over with.

A dim bulb over the kitchen sink created a sickly puddle of light on the floor. I shuffled through the kitchen, trying not to see Chris, perched on the too-small stool at the bar. Shoulders hunched in laughter, plucking hot ginger snaps off a clean white plate. Chris, smiling at his sisters and brothers, sharing some inside joke I'd never know the punchline to. And the shadow of me, sitting in the corner, probably wishing I could go home ... but loving the chance to see Chris so happy, so at home with his own kin.

I don't have time to reminisce!

My legs were healed, but slower ... I tried to move quickly, scissoring my way through the narrow kitchen and following a skinny, dark hallway. I tried not to look

75

at the pictures that lined the hallway ... family portraits, portraits that contained Chris ...

The end of the hallway was like a welcome breath of fresh air. It ended with a stone step down, that led into Bonnie's sunken living room. Two Easy Boy armchairs rested on either side of a creamy suede loveseat. Before Chris's father died, this had been his and his dad's favorite spot to watch football and races on Sundays, according to Chris. I'd often wished I could have met Chris's dad, that perhaps he was nicer than the rest of the family ...

I knew exactly where the ashes would be—on the fire-place mantle.

But as I approached the hearth, I was surprised to see the same old pictures that were always there ... pictures of Chris's father and grandparents. His siblings and their children ... no pictures of me and Chris anymore, I noted. *Well, I can't blame her for that.*

On the center of the mantle, there was a shiny gold water pot that had been passed down for generations: an antique. It had whirls of blue and yellow, fragile patterns of flowers around the trim. If you breathed too close to it, Bonnie would freak.

The first time I met her was right here in this living room. She was smiling then, a sweet, kind, old lady. But now I know she was putting on airs, and when she pointed out the lovely pot, I made a mistake: I reached out and touched it.

Bonnie had grabbed my finger and squeezed. "Oh, no.

You can never touch that. I don't even let my kids do that," she had snapped. The sharpness of her words, the quick-change in her demeanor, had startled me. I'd flushed with embarrassment. But as quickly as she'd snapped at me, Chris had jumped to my defense. "Mom, don't be so uptight. She didn't know ... Jesus."

Bonnie had turned to me and apologized, but her teeth were firmly mashed behind her lips, not used to her son defending another woman against her.

Even now, I didn't dare touch the pot. But there was something else sitting on the shelf beside it, something shiny and new.

A sleek brown box.

When I'd heard that they'd had him cremated, I'd always assumed they'd had his ashes put in a fancy urn, like the ones you see on TV.

But this was just a plain, simple box ... shiny and smooth, it was pretty but nothing special ... *Could this really be Chris?*

Carefully, I stood on my tiptoes and eased the box off the shelf.

I was moving too languidly—only minutes to spare if Bonnie came straight home from town ...

I lifted the box with both hands and stepped back from the mantle. It was surprisingly heavy. Hands shaking uncontrollably, I placed the box on Bonnie's low glass coffee table and, after taking a deep breath, I knelt on the floor in front of it and attempted to pry open the lid.

It didn't budge. To my surprise, the box was sealed tightly shut.

Well, this must be Chris. Has to be …

I lifted the box, carrying it out in front of me like a precious jewel I wanted to keep close, but not too close, and in my head, I could see myself tripping in the dark, Chris's ashes spreading out like a Japanese hand fan all over Bonnie's neat, white carpet … *now that would be my luck.*

I waded through the other rooms, all the while telling myself I was running out of time.

Bonnie's bed was neatly made, a flowery quilt covering it that she'd probably sewn herself. Bottles of perfume and gold-framed photos of Chris decorated her dresser. One of them had been altered—a photo of Chris and I, picking peaches. Only now, the half of the photo that had once contained me, was gone.

I glanced in the bathroom and dining room, taking one last look at the place Chris had once called home. I never appreciated it before, but now … *now*, I wanted to soak it all in.

I stepped outside, carrying the ashes and my duffel bag. The night air felt too hot, too airless all of a sudden …

Carefully, I rested the box on the planter beside the front door while I locked it back up.

As I turned back toward the driveway, I half-expected to see Bonnie standing beside my truck, hands on hips, waiting for me. That disapproving look etched on her face.

But there was nothing but darkness blooming over the truck, still and silent.

Glancing back at the house one more time, I couldn't help thinking that it had once seemed so vibrant, teeming with family, and now it seemed sad and lonely. For a split second, I felt guilty for taking the ashes.

What right do I have? I certainly don't deserve to have them.

But then I remembered how mean they all were, how they wouldn't let me say goodbye to my own husband.

What right did they have to lock me out? ... I was Chris's best friend, not them!

I climbed back inside the truck and secured Chris's ashes on the seat beside me.

Somehow, having him there, felt right.

This time I won't let anything happen to you.

"Remember that road trip we always talked about? Well, better late than never," I whispered. My hands were jittery as I shifted the truck into gear.

Slowly, I descended back down the hill. The tunnel vision returned, the effects of the vodka still pumping through my veins. I couldn't shake the feeling that someone else was driving, taking the wheel from my hands ...

Chapter 7

A flurry of rain pounded the windshield, the wind so wild and vicious, it blew the truck from side to side on the road. I was determined not to slow down, accelerating until I was forced to on account of the hydroplaning.

The radio was staticky, my phone signal drifting in and out, then disappearing completely.

Where am I? It felt like the middle of nowhere, and I would have believed that if not for the heavy Mack trucks speeding up in the two lanes beside me, metal bodies booming like thunder and rattling me from side to side.

I kept waiting for the storm to die down, outside and inside of me, but it never did. Leaving town on a whim was reckless ... not only that, it was *stupid.* And after a few hours on the road, I got the feeling that I was riding *with* the storm, not through it ... that maybe *I* was the cause of the storm, or the storm itself.

Grateful for the GPS on my phone, I let the robotic woman with the British accent guide the way. But once I got to Paducah ... how would I find Valerie? I'd sent nearly thirty messages since she'd asked me to come, but still nothing back from her.

It was three in the morning when I finally forced myself to stop at the first signs of lodging. My eyes were heavy, my head cloudy and thick from the vodka. The short-lived buzz was gone, and now my stomach felt empty and sick. *Leaving home feels like a mistake.*

A sketchy motel with a green tin roof was the only place around for miles. The parking lot was dim, only a couple of cars taking up spaces. I parked and shut the truck off, resting my head on the wheel.

I can't believe I'm so far from home … there's nowhere to hide anymore.

I scooped up my duffel bag, the rattling of pills a welcoming sound. I hadn't taken any pain meds or anti-anxiety meds since leaving Wisconsin. I was long overdue, my entire body achy, my head scratchy.

I picked up Chris's remains, thankful the rain had quit, as I carried him inside, tucked safely under my arm. I shuffled inside the rundown lobby, shivering, my hair and clothes still damp from when I'd stopped at a rest stop earlier.

I'd nearly forgotten about my scars as I approached the sleepy woman at the front desk. Her elbows propped up on the desk top, she was supporting a long, narrow face with a pointy chin and cheeks pocked with old acne scars. Her eyes were heavy with sleep. Like me, she seemed self-conscious of her face, quickly tucking a mound of long orange-red bangs across her face, keeping her cheeks half-hidden.

Her eyes zeroed in on my scars, traveling from the center of my face and down the zig-zag road map that led to my chin. She recoiled slightly, then corrected herself with a tight smile.

"What can I do for you?" She directed her courtesy question at the lumpy, peeling paint on the wall behind me.

I was tired. Too tired to care what she thought about my scars; too tired to be irritated by the way she wouldn't look at me now.

I dropped my bag on the grimy, scuffed tiles at my feet. Gently, I placed the box of Chris on top of it.

"I'd like a room, please. If you have one."

There was a long, awkward pause, and still, she wouldn't look me in the eye.

"Check-out is eleven," she said. Her chintzy gold name tag revealed that her name was Aimee.

"Eleven is fine."

She wasn't wearing a watch, but she glanced down at her wrist and rubbed the pale, exposed spot where one once was. "Listen, it's almost four in the morning. Are you planning to stay for a few days, or ...?"

"Just one night," I breathed, reaching for my wallet. "I need to sleep a couple hours, but I plan on checking out by nine," I added. The room was spinning ... *Too fucking far from home, from the safety of my own itchy walls ...*

The woman leaned over her computer and tapped a few keys. *Hurry hurry hurry, I need my meds ...*

"That'll be 69.18."

82

Dammit.

I thought about my bank account, money dwindling ...
Tick tock tick tock.

I handed her my credit card and minutes later, I was
back outside the grubby motel, climbing an unsteady set of
wet, wrought-iron stairs up to the second-floor walkway. A
row of ten or eleven rooms laid dark, and probably empty.
I shivered again, despite myself.

I struggled with the key card, finally managing to get
the door open on the fourth try.

I was met with a blast of warm air that sent a shiver
through my still-damp hair and clothes.

I set my bag on the bed and put Chris on the nightstand
beside it, sighing. *I can't believe I made it this far.*

Like the lobby, the room was rundown and dreary. A
moon-shaped water stain blossomed on the ceiling above
the queen-sized bed. There was a red-and-black checkered
bedspread that looked faded and worn, and possibly full
of bed bugs ... but I was too exhausted to care at this
point. I kicked off my boots, peeled myself from my jeans,
and stripped off my damp, ragged jacket. Wearing only
a T-shirt, I climbed beneath the covers with my crumpled map and bottles of pills, shivering uncontrollably but
grateful for the dry heat of the furnace.

Paducah, Kentucky isn't far.

I'd never been to Paducah, traveling only once to the
state when I was younger, and that had been to a larger city
called Louisville. I'd gone with Hannah to see a basketball

game. It had been fun, but crowded and hot, and I'd been too nervous to enjoy myself fully.

I was terrible at reading maps, and grateful for my GPS app on my phone. Paducah had been farther away than I'd originally thought—nearly 483 miles. I traced the route I needed to follow with my index finger ... *If only the distance between Valerie and I were as short as it looks on paper.*

I'd knocked out more than half the drive already, reaching Illinois, and if I left at nine, like I'd told Aimee I would, I'd reach Paducah by noon tomorrow ...

But what then?

Even if Valerie was still in Paducah, being held captive by some strange stalker, how could I help her? It wasn't like I'd brought a suitcase full of fancy knives ...

I have no plan, not really. How does she expect me to help her? What can I do?

Pushing the checkered cover aside, I opened my bottles and fished out my pills. I'd gone this long without taking the pain meds, I could probably go without them ... but I took two out anyway, and two anti-anxiety pills. I swallowed them without water, then cringed. Next, I got up and scrambled through my jacket pockets for my phone. I hadn't checked on Valerie in hours, unable to use my phone while driving, and the service had been spotty at best.

The drive itself had gone surprisingly quick; the boxful of Chris beside me strangely comforting despite the storms.

I stared at the box, wondering what Chris would say if he was still alive and knew what I was doing. He'd probably laugh and call me crazy.

I clicked my home button. The screen stayed dark. *Dead.*

I had a charger, but it was hooked up to the adaptor outside in the truck, and the thought of wandering back outside this late in that grimy, poorly lit parking lot gave me the creeps.

I looked around the room, at the few meager furnishings. *I just need to go to sleep. By the time I blink, the sun will be up. And hopefully, Valerie will message me in the morning and let me know her exact location.*

The remote control on the nightstand was sticky. The Bible beside it was sticky, too. I flicked through the pages, my brain buzzing with something I couldn't define ... *was it fear or anticipation?* All I knew was that by this time tomorrow I'd be in Paducah, hopefully tracking down my former classmate.

I rolled onto my side, tucking the itchy blankets up to my chin, and I took another good long look at the box of Chris.

"Oh, don't look at me like that. You know that woman always hated me. I'll return you to her when I get back, promise ..."

When he didn't answer, I leaned over and kissed the smooth, polished surface of the box.

"Good night."

The sound of banging fists on wood shook me from sleep. I sat up with a jolt, blinking sleep from my eyes and absorbing the peeling blue wallpaper and scarred trimmings of my motel room. *I'm in Illinois, on my way to Paducah … and I didn't dream of the accident at all.*

The banging continued.

"Just a sec!" I pulled myself out of bed and grabbed my jeans. They still felt slightly damp and stunk of something rotten and mildew-y.

Hot, dusty streams of morning sun beamed through the cheap curtains, creating shimmery strips of light around the room. *Did I oversleep?*

I wrenched open the motel door, expecting Aimee. Instead, I squinted into the blaring sun at a man around my age. He was wearing overalls and sporting a long, wild black beard. He frowned at me, hands mashed down hard on his hips. "Check-out's eleven, not noon," he barked.

"Oh! Sorry about that. I must have overslept. Give me a few minutes ..."

I closed the door back, cursing myself for having slept so long, and gathered up my bag and jacket. I swiped the pill bottles off the dresser top and buried them deep inside my bag. If I'd had my phone charged up last night, I could have set my alarm.

Much to my dismay, the impatient creep was still waiting outside the door when I came out. I squinted at the harsh afternoon sun, wishing for more storms as I handed him the key to my room. I could feel him watching me, probably checking out my ass, as I climbed down the staircase, taking two slick steps at a time.

I roared out of the parking lot, pissed at the man for being so rude and pissed at myself for oversleeping. I was way behind schedule now ...

It wasn't until I'd made it two miles down the road that I remembered Chris.

"Oh my god! Oh my god!" I was in full-blown panic mode the whole ride back to the crummy motel, all the while praying that the maids hadn't tossed out the box with my husband inside.

Even now, after death, I have failed him.

A cigarette dangled from between my teeth as I slammed the door to my truck and approached a rundown diner called *Pegosi's*. It was well after one; I was three hours behind schedule now after the debacle with Chris's ashes.

Luckily, the room hadn't been cleaned and my dead husband was still in his box where I'd left him.

This time, when I went inside the diner, I left Chris's ashes on the passenger's seat.

He's probably safer without me.

My stomach twisted and curled—how long had it been since I'd eaten? I couldn't remember eating a thing the past two days.

I slid my unlit cigarette behind my ear and pulled up the hood of my sweatshirt. It wasn't enough to conceal my face, but it helped.

Two parallel rows of mismatched tables sat empty. A young girl with a cheek piercing perked up from behind the counter.

"Sit wherever ya like," she drawled. My instinct was the booth in the far corner, furthest from the entrance and the windows. I picked up a plastic, one-page menu from the counter and made my way toward a seat in the middle instead.

The waitress was standing beside a heavy-set man behind the counter. The backline and grill were all out in the open, which should have been comforting, but seemed strange.

They were whispering. *Whispering about me?* I wondered.

Moments later, the waitress came around the counter and walked over to my table, hips shifting sexily from side to side.

She was chewing gum, her eyes focused intensely on mine as she asked me what I'd like. I reached back and adjusted my hood around my face, feeling as though I were under a microscope.

"Steak and eggs, please. Glass of ice water. And coffee, black, if you have some."

"Sure thing." She took the menu from me, then went back to her whispering companion behind the counter.

I stared out the window, which overlooked the parking lot. A couple young boys in a sporty red Camaro zipped in and parked next to the truck. Moments later, they wandered in and chose a table close to me, just as the waitress came floating back with my food. It had taken less than ten minutes to make my brunch, which surprised me.

The desire to turn on my phone and start searching for Valerie ran bone-deep. I'd let it charge for the last hour, and I was hoping—*praying, really*—that I had a new message from her. I forced myself to eat first ... the steak was tough and cold in the center, but the grease and salt were a welcome explosion on my tongue. I leaned my head back and closed my eyes, imagining how good a drink would taste right now—something stronger than water and coffee, at least.

I ate every bit of the chewy meat, barely breathing in between bites, and then I picked at the eggs. My belly was full.

Satisfied, I turned my phone over and stared down at the blank screen. *Please be okay, Valerie. Please let your feed be full of posts, telling your many followers that you were just sick again. That your trip to New Orleans got delayed ... or better yet, let there be pictures ... loads and loads of pictures ... of you doused from head to toe in Mardi Gras beads, sporting one of those icy margaritas, in a cup as big as your head. You don't need my help ... you're fine. Just fine. And I can turn around and go back home, to my prison, where I belong.*

But before I could load my Instagram or Snapchat apps, my phone was chiming and buzzing ... dozens of texts from Hannah pouring in. Several voicemails, too.

What the hell, Hannah? It's been less than twenty-four hours since I sent you a text. Calm down!

The boys were staring over at me, snickering. I gave them the finger and their chuckles rose.

Rolling my eyes, I opened the thread of texts and my breath instantly became lodged in my throat, the room spinning mercilessly.

I tried to focus on Hannah's words, but they blurred before my eyes:

Hannah: WTF Camilla? What the fucking fuck?!!!!!!!!!!!

Hannah: Answer your phone. NOW. Bonnie said you broke into her house. You broke into her house!!!! What the hell were you thinking?

Hannah: You took Chris's ashes from his own mother? And you stole some priceless water pot from her shelf? How could you?? I know you hate the woman ... but how could you be this dumb? TELL ME YOU ARE NOT THIS DUMB.

Hannah: I need you to answer your phone, dammit. I've called you a million times. She's pressing charges. She has an outdoor camera, and guess whose face was all over the fucking thing? YOURS. The police are looking for you, Milly. I'm scared. Please call me.

Panting, I plunged three fingers into my ice water and rubbed cool water over my face.

When had Chris's mother become so high-tech ... installing cameras, that didn't sound like something she'd do ...?

90

The town of Oshkosh already blamed me for Chris's death. Everyone knew I had a drinking problem, and before I "quit", I made frequent trips to Sammy's Spirits and the bar on Melton strip. After stopping, I started driving a couple towns away to buy my alcohol.

For some reason, they didn't test me for drugs or alcohol at the hospital after the accident. *Probably because they thought I was going to die ...*

But everyone suspected I'd been drinking that night, even though nobody could prove it. It was ruled an accident. A horrible, tragic accident. But now they had a reason to nail me. And messing with a dead guy's ashes was no joke in the small, conservative town of Oshkosh ...

My hands shaking, I placed my cigarette in my mouth and flicked my Bic lighter again and again, trying to get a spark.

"Hey! You can't smoke in here, lady." The waitress's polite demeanor was replaced with disgusted concern. She was staring at me, as was the guy behind the counter, and the two young boys. *Do they know what I did?*

"Sorry." I took a twenty out of my wallet and held it up so she could see before placing it down on the table.

I could feel the scars on my face glowing red with shame as I shoved my way out the door. Immediately, I lit my cigarette and stumbled toward the truck, puffing. *I need another drink. Why didn't I save more of those little bottles?*

"Now what?" I said to Chris, as I climbed in behind

the wheel. I rolled my window down, blowing smoke rings out the top of it.

"Now what ..." I mumbled again, glancing back down at the buzzing phone in my lap.

Just as I was about to search for Valerie, it started ringing. *Hannah again ...*

I didn't get a chance to say hello before she started shrieking.

"What the hell, Milly? Seriously, what is going on with you? I know you miss Chris, but you can't break into an old lady's house like that."

"I know. I know! But, listen, I didn't steal that stupid water pot ..." I flicked my half-smoked cig out the window. It bounced off the shiny red car and I felt the corners of my lips threatening to curl up in a smile.

"What? I can hardly hear you," Hannah said, her voice growing louder and louder. I held the phone away from my ear, cringing.

"Where are you?" Hannah shouted.

"I'm in bed. I'm not feeling good ... can I call you later? We can discuss this ..."

"You most certainly are not in bed. I'm standing in your fucking bedroom, Milly!"

Shit.

"The police are looking for you, as we speak ..." Hannah's voice was heated, but also sad. And tired. She was sick to death of her needy, reckless sister. *Me too, Hannah. Me too.*

"Where are you? I'll come pick you up."

I put the truck in gear, glancing briefly over at Chris in the passenger's seat. Now, he was no longer a stupid box, but real ... he raised one mischievous eyebrow at me. *Whatcha gonna do?* He seemed to be saying ...

I put the truck in gear and pulled out of the diner's parking lot. The truck growled as I held the pedal all the way down to the floor. Chris was smiling, as though he approved.

I could still hear Hannah, shouting through the phone on the seat beside me.

Finally, as I veered onto the expressway and hit seventy miles per hour, I ended the call with Hannah. Then I blocked her number, indefinitely.

Chapter 8

The roads were bumpy and stark, storm clouds sprouting like bulgy black bruises in the sky. All the radio stations had evolved into static; an eerie silence hovering between me and the box. The ghost of Chris was gone.

Every few minutes, a howling, old country song would drift through the speakers then fade back out again. I missed the quiet of my apartment, the punchy feel of the keys of my computer ...

But there was something freeing about it, too ... no one knew where I was, no one could reach me if I didn't want to be reached. For the first time, I could see why Valerie enjoyed traveling on her own. Although, unlike me, Valerie had never lost her connection to the world. On the contrary, she kept us apprised of everything going on in her life. *Until now.*

The more miles that stretched between me and Oshkosh, the more the idea of stealing a boxful of ashes and a stupid pot (which I didn't take) seemed small, perhaps even nonexistent … *Is it really a crime to steal your own husband's ashes? If so, it shouldn't be.*

I was starting to see some parallels between Valerie and I; she had her aunt and I had Hannah. Valerie was untethered, unreachable, disconnected from her old life in Oshkosh, and now I was dissociating from that place too. *There are no roots holding me down to the ground. I'm a tree, full of memory rings and scarred from living … but I have no roots to speak of.*

I have no husband to go home to.

But Hannah … *don't forget about Hannah.* A sick, sour curd of guilt was creeping under my skin. *I shouldn't have hung up on her like that. She must be so worried.*

But she wasn't the only one who was worried, I was afraid for Valerie. I was afraid for her life … Although we were never close in high school, we had shared a *moment* once. Valerie, crying in that bathroom stall … even now, I could still imagine the sound of her whimpers, sniffling through the crack in the door …

"Are you okay?" I'd whispered, trying to look through the crack while also looking away. She'd blown her nose loudly, and at first, I thought she hadn't heard me. But then the latch to the door slid open and she motioned me inside.

We were so close in that cramped stall, our elbows rubbing together …

"I lost my dad. After all these years, he's finally fucking dead."

"Oh. I'm sorry, Valerie. I thought you lived with your aunt."

"I did … I do. My dad's a deadbeat, but there was this small part of me that hoped one day he'd get his shit together and come back to get me. Now that's not going to happen."

I climbed onto the toilet seat and cranked open a window.

"Want a smoke?" I'd asked her. Valerie's eyes widened. She was impressed.

We stood there, passing a cigarette back and forth, blowing smoke rings out the tiny crack in the window.

"Thanks for doing this, Camilla."

She knows my name!

"Anytime," I'd told her.

She never gave me the details of her father's death, but I'd heard through the rumor mill that it was drugs. After our moment in the bathroom, I thought perhaps we'd be friends. But the very next day, she was ghosting me in the hallway.

Valerie hadn't messaged me again since leaving Oshkosh. Losing my connection to her should have been a relief, an instant detox … I had an excuse to turn around, run back home. Anyone else would have by now. But a hollow sense of dread had settled in my chest … *There it is again, the silent scream that never comes.*

Something terrible is going on with Valerie, I feel it inside me, like a rattle in my bones I can't shake. What if she hasn't messaged me back because she can't? … Maybe the mystery man in the photos is holding her hostage. And it's not like I can go back now, not with Bonnie and the cops looking for me.

I needed my anxiety pill. I could feel myself getting

the way I always did when I was nervous—fear knocking around my chest, prickly sparks of amped-up adrenaline coursing through my veins like liquid fire. And this hellish town, with its bleak non-scenery, and shitty radio, and no cars for miles ... was starting to freak me out quite a bit.

And Chris was gone ... his fingers like whispers on my skin ...

I welcomed his ghost to return but all I had now was the plain brown box. It didn't feel real that he was inside of it.

The sign for Paducah, Kentucky snuck up on me. It was bright, welcoming, a faded blue tugboat on it.

Tall gray buildings loomed like old tombstones as I entered the Kentucky town. They towered over me, looking down ... their watchful gazes like an accusation.

Paducah reminded me of Oshkosh, only older, but aren't all places the same when you cut them down to the core?

After a while, every person and every place starts to look the same ... like we're all just photocopies of photocopies, one updated version after another ...

But instead of getting updates, I've been getting downgraded.

This is me: version 4.0, series one.

I saw the signs for an elementary school, just as I passed a huge red-brick fire station. The sun was finally making an appearance, sparkling off hundreds of wet windows, reflecting my own bewildered opaque face back at me as I drove through town. A few people were out on the street, their presence a welcome relief. An athletic woman wearing a ballcap and walking a dog jogged across the street in front of me. Crooked sidewalks lined both sides of the street. They weren't crowded, but people were out and about, and the dreary cloud that had hovered over me for the last two days extinguished.

I kept driving, slowing down to let a blue mini-van whir by as I gazed at the buildings and people on the street ... I could almost see her there: shimmery blonde hair with streaks of pink floating around in the wind, big sunglasses perched on her shiny face as she trapezed through the tiny knots of crowds ... *Oh Valerie, if only it were that easy to find you. Tell me where you are!*

The buildings faded away, residential houses puckering out left and right. The houses were small, some more decayed than others.

Two miles outside of the main street, I saw Paducah Primary School perched on the top of a hill. It was a small postage stamp that could have been any small-town school in America. The parking lot was deserted, two yellow school buses parked in the corner.

Across the street from the school, I spied exactly what I'd been looking for: the open, comforting hands of a "safe space", the image of a stack of books ... the Paducah local library.

The truck sputtered and shook as I turned into the nearly empty parking lot of the library.

Back home, our local librarians treated their books and computers like prisoners—you had to sign in, show ID, and produce a local library card just to get near them. I hoped Paducah was a little laxer on their policies. I had ID but no library card ... I prayed they would let me use their computers anyway.

My legs like bowls of jelly, I climbed down from the truck and grunted with pain. My incision sites were achy from the long ride, and my head felt tight, swollen from the inside out. My mouth was watering involuntarily, the way it always did when I was due for a pain pill.

I yanked on the door handle of the library entrance, immediately subdued by the unseasonably cool blast of air conditioning and the woodsy aroma of old, used books. My heart slowed down, my breathing became calmer ... *I'm safe here. No one knows me. Now I can get to work on what I came here for: tracking down Valerie Hutchens.*

A man behind the counter greeted me. He was handsome in a messy way—ruffled black hair too long around his ears and in the back, and a scruffy goatee to boot. Kind, green eyes met mine and for once, I didn't shy away from a man's gaze, although I did pull my hood up over my head. *What must he think of me?*

"May I use one of your computers?" I asked, shyly.

There were a few patrons perusing the shelves, and one teenage girl was using a computer in the corner, but there were several other empty stations.

"Sure." The librarian smiled, studying my face a little too long. He opened his mouth, then closed it and smiled again. I could see it in his eyes: curiosity. *He wants to ask who I am, if I'm new in town …*

Like Oshkosh, Paducah was a small town. *Everybody probably knows each other here, too,* I realized, uncomfortably.

"I'm just passing through town," I said, putting an end to the mystery for him. "Truth is, I'm getting shitty phone service and I need to send out a few quick emails. Would that be okay?" I cleared my throat, my hood slipping down to my shoulders. It was a relief to see that I hadn't forgotten my manners, but it had been so long since I'd interacted with people. *Yet some things do come back, I suppose … like riding a bike or doing a cartwheel.*

"No problem. And I'm sorry about your phone, that really sucks. Follow me." He had a peppy hop in his step, as though he enjoyed his job, and as he led me over to an empty station, I smiled tightly at the young teenager at the computer next to it. Her eyes widened in horror when she saw my mangled face.

"Will this one do?" He pointed at the station beside her.

I found myself liking this man … *Hopefully, everyone in this town is as nice and helpful as he is.*

He had looked at my scars, but he had seen *me*, too. It was a strange feeling, realizing that perhaps my scars weren't all that repugnant, not to everyone at least.

"It's perfect. Thank you."

I took a seat, aware of the teen side-eyeing the lumps and lines on my face. I waited for the librarian to get back to his post before I pulled up Safari. Truth was, I was starting to get a little paranoid about my phone—*What if the cops in Oshkosh were able to track me down with it? There was an app that let you track iPhones, but surely, they couldn't do that, right ...?*

Although every ounce of my being wanted to pull up Valerie's Instagram page, I found myself typing my own name into the Google search bar instead.

I have to know. If the police are really searching for me, I have to know that now.

A sigh of relief passed through my lips as I came up empty on my first try.

But then, I typed in Bonnie's name and searched for Oshkosh crime reports. It was not unusual for Oshkosh to go days, even weeks, without a crime being reported. Unfortunately for me, one had been reported yesterday.

I inhaled sharply.

There I was, nasty scars and all, a bug-eyed side-view of my face ... and it was front and center on page one of the *Oshkosh Gazette*. Hood up around my face, eyes downcast, I stood in the dark on Bonnie's porch, one hand reaching for the door ... in the pale moonlight, my creepy face reminded me of *Nosferatu*.

And the headline said it all: *Caught on Camera, Local Widow Accused of Breaking and Entering, Felony Theft.*

I mashed my teeth together, reading through the lines again and again, until they finally made sense. Horror and fear bubbled inside me, my hands trembling as I forced myself to read it one more time:

Retired teacher, Bonnie Brown, is distraught after she came home to discover a beloved family heirloom and her late son's ashes missing. Luckily, before her son died, he had installed safety cameras outside her home for protection. Much to Ms. Brown's dismay, when she checked the footage, she caught a clear view of the suspect's face, a face not easily mistaken in the town of Oshkosh: her daughter-in-law, Camilla Brown.

Camilla and Christopher Brown were in an automobile accident last Spring, which caused severe injuries to Camilla. Christopher Brown died of his horrific injuries when the vehicle they were traveling in collided with the backend of a semi transporting drainage pipes. The town of Oshkosh is still in mourning over the loss of Chris who was well-liked locally.

When asked why her daughter-in-law would commit such a crime, Ms. Brown said: "My son's former wife has always been unstable. A heavy drinker, she showed up at his funeral intoxicated, so we turned her away. His siblings and I suspected that she was drinking at the time of the accident, but this was never proven. We offered to share the remains, if she wanted to have her own service at a time when she was sober enough to properly mourn my son. She didn't take too kindly to my suggestion, and if you want to know my opinion, these recent acts are all about her getting revenge. I'll be pressing charges, to the fullest extent."

Although one might conclude that these are the words

of a grieving mother, there does seem to be some truth to Ms. Brown's claims. We contacted the driver of the truck involved in the accident. Mitch Reynolds said: "Well, nobody can prove she was drunk when she hit me. But we all suspect it. I could see her flying fast in the rearview, the backend of the Buick fishtailing from side to side. I feel so sad for Chris's mother. It must be heartbreaking to lose her son that way."

Sergeant Brent Matthews said: "All I can say at this time is that we are taking Ms. Brown's report very seriously. Camilla Brown's current whereabouts are unknown, but she is wanted for questioning. Please do not hesitate to contact us if you know where she can be reached. In the town of Oshkosh, we stick together, and we certainly don't desecrate a young man's ashes or victimize upstanding residents, such as Bonnie Brown."

We will follow up with more details on this case as more information comes available.

"That lying bitch," I hissed through my teeth. I scooted back, the metal legs of the chair getting hung up on the thinly carpeted floor of the library and pitching backward. I caught myself, squatting like a football player getting ready to tackle someone, just as the chair hit the floor behind me with a dull thud.

The girl at the terminal beside me widened her eyes and muttered something that sounded a lot like, "Psycho", under her breath.

My eyes fixated on the inky screen and I stared at the reporter's words until they blurred and melted away completely. Suddenly, I couldn't breathe ... *I need to get out of here.*

"You okay?" the librarian called after me as I half-jogged, half-slammed, through the library doors.

Outside, I bent over, hands clutching my knees for support, as I willed my lungs to take in air. *Breathe, dammit, breathe.*

In my sheer panic, I began to count ... an old trick I'd learned from Chris. *Just start counting. Do it. Focus on the shape of the words, don't let your mind go anywhere else.*

I closed my eyes and counted, the memory of Chris on the couch beside me, tracing slow circles on my back to soothe me while I panicked over ... *what had it even been about?* I couldn't really remember.

After the accident, the doctor informed me that I had quite possibly suffered some minor brain damage, and that some memories could be lost. *Was this one of them? I don't want to forget anything that happened between Chris and I ...*

Still counting, I made it to two hundred as the door behind me opened and slammed shut.

From my half-bent position, I glanced over my shoulder, surprised to see the kind librarian again.

"Alright?" he asked, his face stretched tight with concern.

"Just a panic attack. No big deal," I breathed, standing up. Moments passed as we gazed into each other's eyes.

He already knows I'm lying, I realized. And that's when it occurred to me: the article. I'd knocked my seat back and ran out of there like a mindless ghoul ... but I'd forgot to close out the screen.

I took my keys out of my pocket, then dropped them. Stooping down to pick them up, I could feel his heavy gaze on me. *He knows.*

"It's you, right? The girl in the article ...?"

I narrowed my eyes at him, one foot pressed forward. *Ready to run.*

But his expression was soft, worrisome.

"Camilla, right? It's okay. I closed out the screen and logged out your station."

"Why? What'd ya do that for? You don't know me. Why do you care who I am?"

He shrugged. I noticed that his khaki pants were frayed on the ends. His loose-fitting sweater vest scuffed and worn. Something about his casual, but neat, appearance, reminded me of a college professor. *Not that I've ever actually been to college.*

"I was married once." His words threw me off, and then he surprised me further by shrugging a loose pack of Camels from his side pocket. He lit one and handed it to me.

"So?" I took a long drag on the cigarette, instantly hit with the heady rush of nicotine and cancer.

"So, I know what it's like to hate your in-laws. My father-in-law hated my guts."

I watched him struggle to light his own cigarette, his hands shaking as he tried to cup the lighter with one hand to block out the wind.

"Here." I plucked his cigarette from between his lips and used the tip of mine to make fire. "I didn't take the ashes because I hate my mother-in-law. *Former* mother-in-law," I corrected. "And I didn't take that pot they're claiming I took. She's a fantasist. Always has been." I winced, my own words reminding me of hers when she referenced my instability. *Perhaps there was some truth to her words,* I considered.

"I wanted the ashes, that's all. I didn't mean any harm."

He nodded and flicked ash onto the ground. "So, what brings you to Paducah then? Do you have family here, or are you just hiding out?" His eyes floated from my eyes and down to my scars, then back up. For some reason, being seen by him felt like a relief.

"I'm looking for a friend. Her name is Valerie. She was staying in a hotel here on business, and nobody's heard from her for a couple of days. Any idea how many hotels there are in this town?"

He let out a soft, suppressed chuckle that seemed to come from his nose. It was a strange laugh, but I liked it for some reason. I'd never heard one like it before.

"What's so funny?"

"There's only a couple to choose from here. And if she was here on business, and had any sense at all, she probably chose the Marriot on Skyward Drive. I'll give you directions if you want." He poked a finger at the door, encouraging me to come back inside.

"That would be great. Thanks."

Every pair of eyes was on us as we re-entered the library, but I didn't care. For the first time, I had a real lead. If I could find the hotel room from Valerie's pictures and question the staff, I might be able to track down where she went ...

"I'll be right back," I said, as he scribbled down directions on Post-it notes at the counter.

The teenager was gone from the computer area. I bent over the desk, and quickly logged into Instagram. I checked Valerie's profile and my inbox for any new messages. *Nothing. Just as I suspected.*

My phone service wasn't messed up—Valerie just wasn't writing me back ...

A quick scan of the comments on her last post revealed more concerned messages from Aunt Janet.

I can't reach you, Val. Please call me.

Where are you? I'm getting worried.

Checking in again ...

I found no news reports on Valerie Hutchens. *Why hasn't Aunt Janet filed a missing person report if she's so concerned?*

"Here's the address." The librarian was standing behind me again. Quickly, I closed out both screens and shut the computer down.

"Thanks again," I said, standing up and pulling my hood around my face. "I really appreciate your help. And ... your discretion."

"No prob." He smiled and handed me two Post-it notes. One had the address for the Marriott and the other one, a phone number.

"That's my number," he said, tapping it with his finger and looking sheepish. "I'm Lincoln, by the way. Lincoln Smalls. If you need anything."

"Oh." A warm rush of heat lit up my cheeks. *I wonder if my scars are blushing, or if they're still pale and silvery.*

"Thanks. I don't think I'll be here long, though." I tucked the notes inside my pocket and made a beeline for the door.

Chapter 9

As I headed east toward Skyward Drive, it became glaringly obvious that something was wrong with the truck. It was twenty years old and I'd barely driven the thing since my father had passed away. Now, no matter how hard I accelerated, the truck moved slowly and jerkily. It was sputtering and shaking as I merged onto Rockford Lane.

I hadn't changed the oil or had the fluids topped off in the truck since ... well, ever. *It could be the transmission*, I considered, as I revved the gas through a four-way stop and tried to reach 20 mph.

Shit. Don't die on me now, I prayed, stroking the wheel as though it were a person I could coddle and cajole.

I could see the glowing lights of the Marriott on the corner. With a sigh of relief, I clicked my blinker on and coasted down Skyward Drive. The tunnel vision was gone, and now that I was growing used to being behind the wheel again the damn truck was going to die on me.

The Marriott was ten stories tall and looked rather new-ish compared to the surrounding businesses. There was a Dollar Tree, a McDonald's, and a couple of gas stations across the street. *Well, at least I'm not in the middle of nowhere.*

But nothing about this place looked familiar. I tried to recall that night and Valerie's shaky video on the street outside a dimly lit club called *Cavern* ... Unlike the street she'd been walking on, this one was well-lit with a fair amount of traffic. *It couldn't be the same street, could it?*

I turned the truck off, hoping when I came back out, it would be back to running normal.

"Be right back," I said, glancing over at the box of ashes in the passenger's seat.

How strange it is that someone with such a big personality, someone so full of life ... could be reduced to dust particles in a tiny, simple box. Not only is it strange, but it's unfair.

I'm never allowing myself to be cremated, I decided, climbing out of the truck and dusting off my sweaty palms on my jeans.

I'd popped a few of my pills after leaving the library, and although it was probably just a placebo effect, I felt like I could already sense the chemicals flooding my bloodstream ... the cloud around my head was taking shape, reducing my anxiety. *Keeping the scream at bay.*

Inside, there were two women checking in at a long, granite counter. I stood by a fancy fountain, eyeing the shiny round pennies inside it. *Did you make a wish while you were here, Valerie?* I wondered.

There was a sitting area in the lobby, with checkered

fabric armchairs and an oval coffee table stacked with murder mysteries. On the other side of the lobby, was a rich oak bar ... but I didn't need to look to know it was there, the clink of glasses and the smell of barley in the air was enough to wake up my inner-alcoholic.

I imagined myself taking a seat at the bar ... I used to like sitting in the middle, where I'd be more easily seen—and served—by the bartender.

Now, I could almost taste the smooth, fiery flavor as I knocked back shot after shot of tequila ...

"Can I help you?"

An attractive woman with bone-white hair and teeth behind the counter was looking at me. The ladies who had been checking in before me were gone.

I tore my wanting eyes away from the bar, shuffled my hair around my face, and tried to smooth my rancid, rumpled clothes.

"How are you?" I asked the woman, awkwardly.

"Fantastic," she said in a monotone voice that sounded anything but, her lips barely moving as she spoke. "Checking in?"

"No, not exactly. I had a friend who was here recently. Her name is Valerie Hutchens. She was here on business with Rook Pharmaceuticals." I could already see the "I can't give out info" on the tip of her tongue, so I kept talking before she could say it. "You see, it's just that she never made it to her next destination. Her aunt is concerned and so am I. We haven't gotten the police involved yet, but it looks like we may have to. I was hoping you could give me the information I need, and hopefully it's just a big misunderstanding ... some sort of miscommunication ..."

The woman frowned, deeply, her eyes finally raising to meet mine, skimming over my discolored nose and the jagged carnage around it, then floating down to my scruffy clothes and trembling hands. Nervously, I squeezed my hands together to stop them from shaking.

She glanced over my shoulder. *Looking for a boss? Looking for security?* I wondered.

"Spell the name for me. If she's here, I'll let her know she has a guest in the lobby."

I spelled it, forgetting about my hands and tapping my fingers excitedly on my pants.

I looked around the lobby while she checked, desperately searching for Valerie's lovely face ... instead, I came eye to eye with a giggling brunette by the fountain. Her phone was up—*Is she taking a selfie, or is the camera turned towards me?!*

I quickly jerked back around to face the counter, my heart thumping in my chest.

One minute you're walking around, minding your own business. The next, you're on YouTube's Faces of Walmart, or some shit like that.

Stop being so paranoid, I chastised myself, pinching my eyes shut in fear.

"No one by that name is staying here," the woman said, pursing her lips.

My eyes fluttered open. "But she has to be, she told me to come ... unless there's another hotel nearby ..."

The woman shook her head and closed out the computer screen. She rested her hands on the counter primly, waiting for me to leave.

"May I see one of your rooms?" I whined. I could feel the brunette watching, her camera angled right at me ...

"Excuse me?"

"I'm sorry, I appreciate you looking her up for me. But I'm also going to need a room for the night, and I'd like to see what amenities you offer before I choose to stay here."

A family of four with matching *"We are the Whitlocks"* T-shirts and suitcases on wheels came rumbling through the front door. I was relieved to see that the brunette by the fountain was gone.

The Whitlock parents looked brow-beaten and tired. They had that nasally, closed-jaw accent associated with Minnesotans.

"We're all full here. Sorry," the receptionist told me. But she didn't look very sorry.

I stepped aside, letting the family go next. As they booked a room for two nights, I realized that the hotel had room for *them*.

The two Whitlock kids, a boy and a girl, were fighting. The little girl had gapped teeth and a neat French braid; the boy was missing most of his teeth and had a wild cow-tail poking up at the back of his head. The young girl punched her brother in the arm, then he responded in kind—grabbing a fleshy hunk of skin on her inner arm and twisting. She screamed and her mother turned, wide-eyeing the girl and smiling sweetly at the boy.

I could taste the lyrics of that old nursery rhyme on the tip of my tongue ... *What are little girls made of? Sugar and spice. And everything nice.* And the boys ... *snips and snails and puppy dogs' tails.*

The moment we become something other than "sugar and spice", we're no longer worthy, are we?

I winked at the little girl as I wandered back towards the entrance. *No luck here. Dammit!*

Just as I was about to head outside, a group of women emerged from the east hallway, cutting me off. One of them was blonde with colorful highlights, and for a split second, I imagined her face was haunting and beautiful, just like Valerie's ...

I glanced down the hallway from which they'd came, spotting rows of fancy doors. With a quick look back to make sure the receptionist was still distracted by the Whitlocks, I turned right, smiling stiffly at the women as I swiveled around them and walked down the hall.

My nose instantly burned, with that antiseptic smell of chlorine and perspiration that all pools put off. I stopped outside the entrance. There it was: an indoor pool. The glass was steamed up, the water sickly green. Children were squealing.

A memory came floating back to me, tickling the edges of my fuzzy thoughts ... me and Hannah in our neighbor's pool. Dad was pissed because we'd gone over there without permission. He'd held my head down ... too many seconds, too long ... I was trying to scream underwater. *I thought he might kill me that day.*

The hotel pool was surrounded by tables and beach chairs, most of them empty. My eyes zeroed in on a stack of towels resting on one of the chairs—there was a key card sitting on top of it. I scanned the water, looking for the hotel guest it belonged to.

A young, red-headed mother was in the pool, frantically trying to keep up with two small children in floaties—they both looked to be under five.

Decidedly, I pressed the door and walked inside, grateful it wasn't locked.

The mother turned her head toward me for a split second, then one of the children squealed and she was thrashing through the water after him.

I bent down in front of her chair, pretending to tie my shoes. Before I could change my mind, I reached over and swiped her key card, stuffing it inside my pocket.

I used the key card to open room 104, which was thankfully, on the first floor. I'd passed a maid and a few other guests on the way, but luckily, I hadn't seen that snooty receptionist.

As I opened the door, I was hit with a blast of cool air and country-apple air fresheners. I closed the door back behind me, silently praying the father of the two brats wasn't somewhere inside this room. *If so, I'll just pretend to be a maid,* I decided.

There was a king-sized bed draped with a red-rose comforter in the center of the room. A couch and love-seat adorned with rose-petal patterns to match. Children's clothing and toys were scattered all over the room.

The windows were draped in heavy red curtains from floor to ceiling. It looked like it could have been a white room once, but then it got covered in blood spatter.

But only one thing mattered: it looked nothing like the hotel room in the background of Valerie's video.

No, this isn't the hotel she stayed at.

I imagined Valerie behind the camera lens in her video, her pasty white face and darkly hooded blue eyes. *She was sitting at a desk. The walls were white. The comforter and drapes were white, too …*

This isn't it. Doesn't look anything like it. There's not even a desk in this room …

I turned to go, feeling completely helpless and stupid for breaking into someone's room, and that's when I saw it—a half pint of rum beside the bed. *Mama's midnight snack, to take the edge off.*

It was half empty already, but I scooped it up and stuffed it in my duffel bag before leaving. I dropped the key card on the floor, hoping she'd think she left it behind when she'd gone to the pool.

On my way back outside, I closed my eyes and breathed deeply as I passed the bar. I didn't have to look to know that someone was drinking a martini. It smelled like fat juicy cherries and salty green olives, and if I tried just a bit, I could taste them in the back of my throat.

I can't wait to taste this rum.

Back in the truck, I couldn't wait anymore—I twisted the lid off the bottle, lifting it to my lips. As I finished it off, my phone chimed. A message from Valerie!

I'm staying at The Rest EZ. Pls hurry. I'm scared.

I drove until I saw a sign for Preston Court, my heart thumping in anticipation. I'd looked up the directions for *The Rest EZ* online, and it was only nine blocks from the Marriott.

The buildings on Preston were rundown, some of them boarded up. There was a billboard for "Girls Girls Girls" and a casino in thirty miles. I would have missed *The Rest EZ* if I hadn't been looking for it. It was set back from the road in a gravel parking lot. A long, one-story building, it was lined with yellow, numbered doors. Every car in the lot looked broken down, or barely running.

I parked at the first yellow door, the only one that wasn't numbered.

I sent a message to Valerie. **I'm here. What room are you in?**

Drumming my hands on the steering wheel, I watched ten minutes tick by on the clock. *Where the hell is she? Why won't she write me back?*

Desperate, I emerged from the truck and approached the first door. The motel—if you could call it that—was seedy and rundown. *Why in the world would Valerie stay here? Surely, Rook paid for her lodgings …*

"Manger" the first unnumbered door read, in chubby gold letters on a paper sign taped to the door. I knocked, softly.

I glanced around the mostly empty lot, looking for signs of life as I waited for someone to answer. The air was cool and quiet, and there was an eerie, abandoned fog surrounding the rundown place. I took a breath and rapped again on the *Manger's* door.

This time, I heard a cough, and what sounded like someone moving heavy bits of furniture around, then the door swung open.

A man wearing sweats and a stained T-shirt appraised me. There was a glass of what looked like water, but smelled like ass, with pulpy bits of fruit in the bottom, in his left hand. My mind instantly returned to the now empty bottle of rum in my bag.

"How can I help you, miss?" He scanned me with his eyes, barely glancing at my mottled face as his eyes moved down to my chest and waistline. He smiled, the smell of that rotten drink emitting from his mouth and pores.

I was reminded of some childish game I used to play but couldn't quite remember … *Now, take one giant step backward.* I backed up a few steps from the drunken man, trying not to breathe in his fumes.

"I-I'm looking for someone. A friend of mine who's staying here. Her name is Valerie Hutchens."

He didn't react to her name, only took a slow sip from his drink. "What room's she in, hon?" he asked, and I could see small shreds of fruit stuck between his teeth.

"I'm not sure, but I can show you what she looks like."

I dug my phone out of my pocket, flipped to her Instagram page and held up a photo. The man squinted at the screen.

"Yep. She was here. But I haven't seen her in a couple days. Left with her boyfriend, I think. Are you here to clean out the rest of her stuff?"

"Her boyfriend? Was someone staying with her?" I asked, my heartrate speeding up as I imagined the creep in her window.

"Well, I didn't think no one was ... but he's the one who paid the bill, so I guess. They were supposed to check out today, but I guess they left early." He shrugged. "Listen, people around here value privacy, and I like to give 'em just that. I don't know anything about her, and I don't know anything about him either."

"Did you see her in the car when they left? What were they driving? She told me she was here. I can't see why should would tell me that if she wasn't ..." I was rambling, my mouth thick and sticky from the rum. I looked over my shoulder at the few beat-up cars that were parked there.

"Nah. I never saw her leave. Never saw him leave either ... it was a red car, I think. But like I said, I'm not a snoop ..."

I stared beyond him into the mangy motel room. Although it looked like a regular old room from the outside, this particular room was used as an office. There was a small computer and dented metal desk in the corner. A box TV set and beat-up loveseat sat in the center of the room.

"Are you the manager?"

The man narrowed his eyes at me. "Sure am. That's what the sign says, don't it? I also live here. My digs are right next door. Your friend was in the very last room over there, number 14. Now, that's all I know. She's not here now, so ..."

"May I stay in that room? I'll clean up anything she left behind. She might be planning to come back ... she told me she was still here ..."

I expected him to refuse me, but he opened the door and waved me inside.

I leaned my back against the metal desk while he chicken-pecked at the keys.

"I'm assuming the man who paid for my friend didn't leave a name or credit card info behind? Possibly a copy of his ID?" I asked.

"Can't say that I recall. I'm pretty sure it was cash. Even if I had a card on file, I wouldn't give you that information, lady. And I don't make copies of driver's licenses. That's elusive."

I wanted to correct him—*intrusive*—but held my tongue.

"Now, here's the room key. It's fifty bucks a night. You can pay when you check out." He thrust a stiff plastic card at me, with the number 14 engraved on it.

"Yes, sir," I said, with a tight smile. "Was this the guy?" I held up the phone again, this time using the photo of the Chris lookalike at the concert in Ohio.

He shook his head, but I noticed that he'd barely looked. *Even if it was him, would this guy tell me? Probably not,* I realized. He was certainly being less than helpful.

"Are you sure?" I pressed.

"I didn't really pay attention to the guy. I don't stare at people. Staring's rude, ya know?" He stared straight at me, his eye twitching as he got a good look at my scars.

I was barely out the door before he closed and locked it behind me.

Chapter 10

Rooms two through thirteen were closed, no guests poking their heads out as I followed the exposed pathway that led toward Valerie's former room—*my* room now—on the opposite end of the *Manger*'s room. Nobody was standing outside talking or smoking, no cars pulling in or out. My footsteps echoed down the skinny walkway, a shiver running from the base of my spine all the way to my scalp. *Why would Valerie ask me to come here if she's not here?*

Away from the main business strip in town, this place felt like a ghost-town. But as I reached room 12, I could hear music playing inside, a familiar song—*I Just Want to Sleep* by Nirvana.

So, I'm not alone with the fruit-man, after all. I was starting to feel like a guest at the Bates Motel. "Where the hell are you, Valerie?" I mumbled under my breath.

Before letting myself in the room, I sent yet another message:

I'm here. Where are you? I'm getting worried. The

manager said you left with some guy ... you're coming back, aren't ya? Why are you scared? Tell me what's going on.

I stared down at the message for a few seconds, then clicked send.

Slowly, I opened the door to room 14. It was dark inside.

I stepped in and closed the door back behind me. I dropped my bag and stumbled around, flipping on every light switch I could find. *This place is too fucking quiet.*

A queen-sized bed with an off-white comforter sat in the center of the room. The bed was unmade.

To the left of the bed was a wooden desk. To the right: a window with long, billowy curtains that looked white at first glance, but were stained with several years' worth of nicotine and dust.

I stared at the desk. *If I were sitting there, the bed would be behind me ... and the window ... the window where the man was looking in. This is it—this is the room she was in when she made the video.*

Seeing Valerie's hotel room in-person was different than seeing it in the video. The room had looked glamorous, but only because she had been sitting inside it, and only because that's what I had expected to see. In reality, the room was shit. The carpet was brown and frayed, the air moldy with old smoke and something else ... rotten food, maybe?

The manager had mentioned her "stuff" she'd left behind, but I couldn't see what he meant. I ventured further into the room, holding my breath.

In front of the bed, there was a stand with a small smart TV and a mini-fridge built in below. I opened the fridge, surprised to find Styrofoam leftover boxes and two half-drunk bottles of Vitamin Water.

I took one of the bottles out and gripped it in my hand, trying to imagine Valerie standing in this exact same spot ... her lips soft as rose petals caressing the mouth of the bottle ...

Sighing, I put the water back and closed the fridge. Down a short hallway, there was a small bathroom. The mirror above the sink was smudged with what looked like fingerprints. There was a soft pink toothbrush beside the sink, and a bottle of hair spray. I found a damp black T-shirt draped over the shower bar and a sponge hanging on the hot-water nozzle.

Valerie is gone. I know she's gone because this can't be all her stuff. A T-shirt and a toothbrush? I don't think so. Valerie probably travels with a huge suitcase stuffed with makeup and other beauty supplies. Her T-shirt is still damp ... surely, that means she hasn't been gone that long ...

I stared at my face in the mirror, fingers brushing across the scars I'd never get used to. *Did Valerie stare at herself in this mirror, too? Oh, how it must feel to look in the mirror and like what you see ...*

But Valerie wasn't the only one who liked what she saw ... she also had an admirer.

I went back to the window. There were no blinds, only the drab, semi-see-through curtains, and through the window pane, I was startled by what I saw.

An empty field behind the hotel, and beyond that, wild trees and shrubbery grew around what looked like remnants of old state fair equipment.

A rusty old Ferris wheel glittered in the distance— it wasn't huge, like some I'd seen, but a small-ish one that you might see at a county fair. There was another dilapidated metal contraption, too. It looked like a spider, with spindly metal legs; the tip of each crooked leg was a bucket seat for someone to ride in. They obviously hadn't been used in years; roots and tree limbs growing all around them like they were trying to consume the old rides ...

Why the fuck would Valerie stay in this creepy-ass place? I wondered. *Nothing about this makes sense.*

I gulped down a handful of meds, swallowing them with water from the sink.

I sat on the bed, my mind whirling like that old, creaky Ferris wheel out back.

What should I do now? She's obviously not here. And although my intentions were good, I couldn't help feeling like *I* was the creep, coming here on a whim.

But she told me to come ... although I still don't know why ...

I kicked my boots off and stretched out on the bed. With my head on the soft white pillow, I willed Valerie's previous thoughts to seep through the fibers and drift into mine ... *Tell me where you are so I can help you.*

I glanced over at the window again, instantly chilled at

the thought of someone watching her ... watching *me* ...

If some psycho followed her from that bar, he easily could have hidden behind the building and watched her ...

And since room 14 was on the end, it would have been easy to slide around the curl of the building and break into the room. *Or hell, maybe he just came in through the window.*

The window had been open, because I'd seen the curtains rustling in the breeze behind her. And that face ... he was standing right there, staring in at her ... quietly waiting, watching ...

I searched for a bar called *Cavern* on my phone but came up with nothing. *It can't be far from here. Maybe that's where she went?*

The sun was setting outside the window, dusk settling over the already dark field behind the motel. The thought of going out and walking down this deserted stretch of road in search of that bar by myself was terrifying.

I instantly thought about the man I'd met earlier today ... Lincoln. Compared to the weirdo manager, he seemed like a decent person to ask to accompany me.

Feelings of guilt rose up ... *Why do I feel guilty? Because I'm going to ask another man to take me to a bar so I can try to find my friend?*

I stood up and went over to my bag, removing the box of Chris's ashes once more. "You'd rather me go there with someone, right? To make sure I'm safe?"

I set the box on the bedside table, my mind wandering

back to the mystery man in the window. *Who is he? And what does he want with Valerie?*

And if a man paid Valerie's bill, did he take her with him? A terrible thought was licking at my brain ... *What if he hurt her ... killed her? What if I was too late?*

I laid back on the bed, the room spinning as it usually did when my meds first kicked in. The pain pills dulled the physical and emotional pain; the anxiety pills quieted the scream inside me. And it had been so long since I'd last taken my dose ... *or did I take a dose earlier?* For some reason, I couldn't remember. *I'm losing track, taking too many sometimes, and other times, not enough. Just like I did with the booze.*

I clutched my phone to my chest, wishing—*willing*— Valerie to respond. Finally, I sent a message to Lincoln: **Hey, it's Camilla. We met at the library today. Could you take me to a bar in town called Cavern? lmk.**

The next time I opened my eyes, it was completely pitch-black outside the motel room. I jolted up in bed, too fast, my head spinning. The lightbulb in the lamp beside the bed flickered once, then twice.

What time is it? I wondered, groggily.

Remembering the text I'd sent earlier, I reached for my phone that had fallen on the floor beside the bed.

It was almost ten. Valerie had still not written me back. *Where the fuck is she?!*

However, I did have a message from Lincoln. He'd sent it nearly two hours ago ...

Lincoln: Sure, what time?

Fuck.

I wrote back quickly:

Me: Hey, so sorry. I fell asleep at the motel. I'm at The Rest EZ. You know it? I was tired from driving, I guess. You still awake? Want to make a late-night trip to that bar, Cavern? My friend might be there ... I'm hoping I can find out more information about her whereabouts. I know it's late, so if you can't, I understand.

I felt lost as I looked around the motel room, the fog that often accompanied waking up after overmedicating hanging around my head like an invisible bubble. *How many pills did I take?*

I picked up my pill bottles and twisted off the caps. Three shiny white pills rattled around inside. I turned the bottles on their sides and read the labels.

No refills.

I haven't been to see Dr. Norris in almost three months ... I wonder if I call her, maybe she'll refill ...?

But I already knew the answer to that: even if I did have more refills, it wouldn't be time yet to fill them. I'd been taking too many lately, not considering what I'd do when I ran out ... some days forgetting to take them completely, while other days popping two or three at a time to compensate for the missed dose. They used to make me feel relaxed, less sad ... but now ... now I just take them not to feel like shit, really.

Somewhere between the sheets, my phone was buzzing. I wrestled with the blankets, practically pouncing on the phone when I saw it.

"Hello?"

"Um ... is this Camilla?"

I smiled, instantly recognizing Lincoln's soft-spoken voice on the other end.

"It's me. Look, I'm sorry for texting back so late. I fell asleep."

Lincoln coughed loudly on the other end, and I wrenched the phone away from my ear until he was done.

"That's alright. I was still awake." But I could tell by the phlegm in his throat and the foggy shape of his words that he'd just woken up.

"You still want to go? I can be there in ten or fifteen minutes ... listen, don't walk down there. That's not the nicest part of town. I thought you were going to stay at the Marriott?" He was nervous, rambling, and for some reason, I was smiling cheesily, as I balanced the phone between my ear and shoulder. I shimmied my boots onto my feet.

"Yeah, if you're up for it. I'm in room 14. I came here because this is where my friend was staying, the one I told you about ... but she's not here. I can't figure out where she is."

"Oh." He sounded far away for a moment, then his voice was muffled on the other end. "See you soon, Camilla."

I hung up, my heart knocking around in my chest. It seemed stupid, crazy, to trust a stranger. But he was a librarian. *Librarians are trustworthy, right?*

Under the headache-inducing phosphorescent lights in the bathroom, I brushed my teeth and rubbed some powder onto my cheeks. It wasn't enough to cover up the scars, but it helped a little bit.

I pulled a raggedy Bengals sweatshirt over my head. If I'd had nicer clothes, I would have brought them … but ever since the accident and the bloating weight gain from my meds, I couldn't fit into much besides old tops and pants. My face had gone to shit, and now my mind and body were, too.

I was just stepping outside to smoke when a royal-blue Jeep came rumbling through the parking lot, kicking up gravel dust.

I stared into the blinding headlights as the Jeep parked right in front of my room. When the lights popped off, I was relieved to see Lincoln's face, although some part of me was hoping it was Valerie.

Lincoln looked wide awake now, his hair shiny and combed neatly to one side. When he got out, I noticed that he looked different from how he had at the library, more relaxed. He was wearing loose-fitting stonewashed jeans and a plain white T-shirt. Through his shirt, I could see curls of dark chest hair and a muscular torso. I looked away, blushing.

"How are you?" he asked, looking me in the eye like a normal person.

I stubbed my cigarette out, fingers jittery.

"Fine. I need to grab my ID and cash."

A few minutes later, we were pulling away from *The Rest EZ*, drifting down the poorly lit, mostly abandoned street.

"What do you know about *Cavern*?" I asked him, scanning the broken sidewalks lining each side of the street, looking for Valerie's ghost in the moonlit shadows.

"Me?" Lincoln sounded surprised by the question. "Next to nothing, really. I've never been there. I've only lived in Paducah for a few years now. I've heard about it, but I don't think it's all that popular."

"Definitely not the kind of place you meet doctors or health associates to wine and dine them and discuss your latest drug products, right?" I asked, the question more to myself than to him.

"I don't think so," Lincoln said, tentatively. "Are you sure that's what she was here for?"

"I'm not really sure of anything these days," I said.

He made a hard right turn into a quiet industrial complex. Through an open gate, he parked in front of a solid gray building with no cars out front.

"It's here, or it's supposed to be ..."

For the second time in the past few hours, I thought to myself: *This place is too fucking quiet.*

"Why do you think this is it?" I asked, suddenly hesitant to be in the car with a stranger, but also hesitant to step out into the empty, dark lot.

He looked over at me, his cheeks reddening. "I called a friend of mine and asked. I'm not much of a partier, but he told me it was here."

"Well ... I guess we could get out and look," I said, doubtfully.

"You want to stay here while I check it out?" Lincoln offered.

I shook my head. As chivalrous as his offer was, the thought of staying in the Jeep by myself was nerve-racking too. "I want to go."

I wrenched the door to the Jeep open, and together, we approached the two steel doors. There were no signs on the doors, no indication that this place was anything other than an old industrial building not in use.

Lincoln tugged on the door. "Locked."

I tried the other door (also locked) while he took out his phone and started texting. A few minutes later, he said, "Okay, I just asked Tommy. I think I got it. Follow me."

I followed him around the side of the building and down a skinny alleyway littered with cigarette butts and broken beer bottles. Finally, we stopped side by side at the top of a stone staircase that seemed to lead down to some sort of basement or cellar beneath the building.

"This is where we go in," he said.

"You sure? Where are all the cars?" I said, looking around the empty alleyway, nervous.

I couldn't shake the feeling I'd had earlier of being at the Bates Motel. Only now, this was starting to feel like something scarier, like I was heading down to some sort of serial killer's secret dungeon.

"I don't know," Lincoln said. "I'll go first." Slowly, I

descended the stairs, sticking close to his backside. At the bottom was another closed, steel door. I expected it to be locked.

"Let's hope this one opens. Or … maybe it's better if it doesn't," I muttered under my breath. But now that we were standing in front of it, I could hear the unmistakable thrum of music on the other side of the door.

Lincoln opened the door with ease, and I followed him into the darkness.

Chapter 11

The first thing the beefy, bald bouncer did was ask for the keys to the Jeep.

"It's illegal to park out there. Valet will move you to the lot next door. Here's your ticket." He thrust a small paper ticket, the size of a Chuckie Cheese stamp, into Lincoln's outstretched palm.

Lincoln pocketed the ticket and glanced back at me, warily. He looked just as sketched out as I felt.

Together, we winded through a dark, narrow hallway that opened into a massive room with exposed pipes and beams overhead. I was shocked to find the floor crowded with people—more people than I ever could have imagined lived in Paducah. A cloud of smoke rose through the crowd, either from cigarettes or fog machines, I couldn't tell.

Electronica music boomed from the speakers, vibrating my back and brain. People were dancing or standing around in clusters, some nicely dressed in business-y attire, others in casual shirts and jeans. A double-sided bar extended the entire length of the room; on one side of the bar, there were girls in black shorts and lacy, black bras dancing, and on the other side, a man with a mohawk and a girl with a stubby black ponytail were serving drinks.

We stood at the edge of the dance floor, staring. The lighting was strange, coating the patrons' skin in a green, ghoulish light and making their teeth ultra-white. I couldn't imagine what it was doing to my scars ...

"Wow. Just wow." Lincoln was standing beside me, surveying the room with shock. "I had no idea this was here," he said, his eyes and teeth so white they were blinding.

"Best-kept secret in Paducah, honey," came a purr from behind us. A girl with long, dark braids, wearing what looked like a latex suit, swooped in front of us. She was carrying a tiny tray of neon-green Jell-O shots. She held them under our noses like miniature Christmas presents.

"Care for a shot, darlin'?" she directed this question at me.

"No, thank you." It seemed strange, refusing a drink when asked, but then again, I'd never been much of a Jell-O shot person.

"Want to get a drink at the bar? Maybe ask the bartender if he's seen your friend ...?" Lincoln suggested.

"Sure. Okay," I said, giving the waitress an apologetic smile.

Lincoln took my hand, his palm like a slippery wet fish in my fingers. He led the way, weaving through the crowd and keeping me connected to him.

It had been over a year since I'd been inside a bar, and I'd never really been in one sober. I had always been the nervous type ... the kind of girl who drinks too much *before* she makes it to the bar in the first place.

The whole place felt alive, electricity in the air, my chest and back vibrating in tune with the music.

Lincoln found an open spot and signaled the man with the mohawk. I couldn't take my eyes off the dancing girls on the other side, their shorts cutting off right below their bottoms, long, tan legs smoothed to perfection. Most were dark-headed, but one was blonde. She whipped her hair side-to-side like a shampoo commercial, lost to the rhythm of the song, and for a brief moment I imagined it was Valerie up there, magnetizing the room with her whiplash hair and haunting charisma ...

"You have her picture?" Lincoln shouted, trying to reach me over the music. He was watching me watch the girls, giving me a funny look. Numbly, I nodded.

"What can I get you guys?" The bartender approached us, not smiling. He looked distracted, angry, or both. His eyes were scanning the room behind us. *Probably averting his eyes from my scars,* I thought, self-consciously. I couldn't imagine how pronounced they were under the heady glow of the lights ...

I yearned for the safety and solitude of my own house.

"I'll take a Jack and Coke. What do you want?" Lincoln nudged me.

"Oh." I should have prepared for this. But maybe, deep down, I knew this was coming.

Order a soda. Order a soda. Order a soda, I repeated in my head.

"Sprite with a splash of vodka," another version of me told the man.

"Splash of vodka," the bartender repeated back to me, then turned around to make our drinks.

"When he gets back, we'll ask him about your friend," Lincoln said, hopefully. My eyes were glazing over, the shiny glass bottles behind the bar blurring together as one ... Lincoln was still watching me, his eyes etched with concern.

"Yeah. Let me find the photo." I dug around for my phone and found the same picture of Valerie I'd shown to the motel manager. *What were the chances someone would recognize her in here?*

When the bartender returned carrying our drinks, my mind was so focused on the shiny glass tumbler, that Lincoln had to nudge me again to show him the pic.

"Excuse me," I leaned in and shouted over the music, "I'm looking for this girl. Have you seen her?" I held up her picture on my cell phone.

The bartender frowned, looking around at all the waiting customers crowding in behind us. He glanced at Valerie's picture, his face morphing instantly. His eyes turned soft. "Yeah, I saw her here. She's kind of hard to miss, you know?"

Yes, I do know.

"Is she here now? When did you see her?" I asked, excitedly.

The bartender shrugged. "Days ago. Maybe Monday or Tuesday? Not sure."

"Who was she with? Do you know?" I asked, my heart sinking with disappointment.

"She was in the VIP section with several guys from Whole Spring. She came up to the bar a few times to get beers. She was sweet. I think she said she was a traveling nurse or something ..."

"A pharmaceutical rep," I corrected him. "You said she met with some guys from Whole Spring. What is Whole Spring exactly?" My mind instantly conjured up a picture of the *Whole Foods* store back home.

"Mental health clinic in town," Lincoln said quietly in my ear.

"Did she leave with those guys?" I pressed.

The bartender shook his head, clenching his jaw in annoyance.

"Look, she's missing. She was staying in a motel up the road from here, but now she's gone. She said that she thought someone from the bar followed her back to her room the other day ..."

I could see Lincoln's mouth fall open in surprise in my periphery. This was more information than I'd given him, but what did he expect? I didn't know him well enough to share all the details yet ...

The bartender looked less surprised.

"Well, I couldn't see anyone from around here hurting a girl like that ... but I do know one of the guys she was with from Whole Spring. We went to high school together. His name is Aaron. He comes in occasionally, but not very often. You might check with him and see if he knows anything ... other than that, I don't know how else I can help you ..."

"What about this guy? Have you seen him?" I held up the smudgy photo of the Chris lookalike from the concert.

The bartender rolled his eyes. "No."

"The other bartender? Might she know anything?"

"No, she only works two days a week. Listen, I got other customers to help." He pointed at the man in line behind us.

I took that as our cue to move on.

"Wait. I'll grab our drinks," Lincoln said, but I was already pushing my way through the crowd, trying to find an open chunk of space to breathe in.

Moments later, Lincoln spotted me and smiled. He was carrying his Jack and Coke in one hand, my vodka and Sprite in the other.

I could already taste the vodka on my tongue.

"Here." He slipped the ice-cold glass into my hand and instantly, I was tipping it back, the rim settling comfortably between my lips.

The vodka went down smoothly and bloomed like a fire flower in my chest.

One sip is enough. But one sip was never enough, not for me, just like one pill wasn't enough either. I finished off the drink and thrust it back at Lincoln. "Can we get out of here, please?"

He looked surprised, only just now lifting the whiskey glass for his first taste.

"Do you want to sit down? You looked peaked," Lincoln said.

"No. Can we just go outside? I can't breathe in here."

"Sure. Of course." Lincoln downed half his drink, then motioned for me to follow him back out. The bouncer looked irritated to see us again so soon.

My hands were shaking from the vodka as I held up my phone with Valerie's picture on it in front of the bouncer. "My friend was here several nights ago. The bartender with the mohawk saw her. She's gone missing. And she said someone followed her home from here the other day ... have you seen her?"

The bouncer stared at the photo of Valerie, his tough mask never slipping. "Nah, never seen her before ..."

"Are you sure? The bartender mentioned she was with some guys from Whole Spring?"

The door to the club swung open. Two young girls, who looked barely old enough to vote, stumbled into the club. They were holding out their phones—once again, I felt like they were pointed at me, at my cluster-fuck of a face.

"Move along," the bouncer barked at us.

I mumbled an awkward "Thanks" as he let us back through the door.

Up the steps and back outside in the chilly air, I was

surprised to see tiny snowflakes falling from the sky. We followed the alleyway back out to the parking lot. I glanced at the empty spot where the Jeep once was.

"Shit. I forgot to get my keys back from the guy at the door ..." Lincoln said.

"I think it must be parked over there." I pointed across the street, to a dimly lit parking garage. "I'll wait here."

Shakily, I lit a cigarette while Lincoln jogged back down the alley and disappeared back inside the cavernous nightclub.

It was just one drink. Well, two, if you count that little shot bottle the other day ... oh, and there was the rum ...

But somehow, it felt like so much more ... like something old and horrid had crept back into my heart and taken refuge there. *Something that had never left in the first place ...*

"Alright?" Lincoln was back with the keys, shaking them and smiling. I could tell he wasn't drunk, but there was an edge to his voice from the whiskey.

"I'm okay."

"You were right. It's over there," Lincoln pointed toward the garage.

Together, we crossed the dark, empty parking lot, neither of us talking for several minutes.

"I shouldn't have brought you here. I read the article. I know there was alcohol involved in your accident. I don't know what I was thinking ..."

"Lincoln, stop. I'm the one who asked you to bring me, remember? And I'm the one who ordered the drink."

I kept going, eager to get back to the motel room and

think. *Maybe when I get back, Valerie will be there,* I thought, hopefully.

"I know what it's like to have scars," Lincoln said, catching up with me. I stopped and whipped around to look at him. His face was soft and smooth, shiny like a marble countertop. All his limbs were intact. *What the fuck does he know about scars?*

As though he could hear my thoughts, he said, "I was stationed in Iraq for six years. I moved to Paducah after I got discharged, to take care of my mom, and because my wife wanted a divorce. Mom was sick with Alzheimer's. She died last year."

"Oh. I didn't know. I'm sorry," I said, quietly.

"Don't be. We all have things that leave scars. Some visible, some not. I had PTSD really bad when I first got home, and I couldn't take care of my mom properly … and I couldn't blame my wife for wanting someone else. I wasn't who I used to be anymore."

"I'm sorry," I said again, feeling like one of those robots commenting on Valerie's page. "You don't look anything like how a soldier is supposed to look …"

Lincoln laughed, that nasally giggle of his.

"Maybe that's the point. I wanted to do something different, be someone else after I got better," he said.

I nodded.

"Camilla, your scars aren't bad. I can tell you hate them and that you try to cover them up. But I think you look beautiful just the way you are."

"I don't hide them." But we both knew that was a lie.

"Sometimes hiding is good ... it helps us heal. I turned into myself for a long while, put up all these walls around me, to shield myself from the world and to keep the world from seeing how fucked up I was after the war."

"What changed? How did you get better?" I asked, curiously.

"I went to therapy. Talked to people. Went through the motions of life until they stopped feeling like motions. And I still struggle with it ... but for some reason, when I first saw you, and then I read that article ... I don't know, you just felt like someone I needed to know. Like someone who'd been through something like me. Does that make sense?"

"Kind of," I said.

"This Valerie person ... is she your person? I mean, does she help you deal with the trauma from the accident and ... and your husband's death?"

I squeezed my lips together, thinking about my online chats with Valerie. *Had we ever discussed anything of substance? No, not really.*

Part of me wanted to let the truth spill out, but it all sounded so crazy in my head.

I nodded. "I guess she is. Let's get back. I'm cold."

Lincoln draped his black leather jacket over my shoulders, which seemed ridiculous and cheesy, but it was thick and warm and smelled like cinnamon.

"Through here." We ducked under a low overhang and

143

entered the parking garage. By the time we made it to the third level, my legs were burning, and I was out of breath. The vodka burned in my chest, heating up my cheeks and making my head swim gloriously.

"You okay?" Lincoln asked for the third time as he held open the passenger's door of the Jeep for me.

"Fine," I huffed. We were quiet on the ride back to the motel. *Too fucking quiet.*

"So, what's the plan?" Lincoln asked as he parked in front of my motel room. There were no new cars in the lot—no sign of Valerie in sight.

I unbuckled my seatbelt and put my hand on the door handle.

"What plan?"

"For finding your friend. You said someone followed her back to her motel room. Don't you think you should file a police report, or something, if she's missing?"

"I'm going to find out more about this Whole Spring first. Maybe go there in the morning and see if I can talk to that Aaron guy the bartender mentioned. Maybe he knows something. Or maybe one of the other guys that works there does ..."

Lincoln chewed on his lip, thoughtfully. "You sure you don't want to grab a bite to eat tonight, or meet in the morning? I could take you over to Whole Spring on my way to work?" he pressed.

I shook my head, thinking of Chris-in-the-box, waiting for me inside.

"I can take it from here. Thanks for taking me to the bar though. And I'm sorry I kind of flaked out back there."

"It's no problem, really. You sure you don't want me to go with you tomorrow?"

I shook my head again. He was trying too hard, and it made me feel bad. "I'm sure, Lincoln. You've done enough already."

I gave him an awkward wave and stepped out, closing the door of the Jeep behind me. He waited, watching me unlock the door and go inside. I listened on the other side, waiting until I heard him pull away.

A strange feeling of guilt bubbled inside my belly. *I don't know him. Why does it matter if I disappointed him?*

But that's all I'd been doing lately—disappointing everyone around me. *After a while, you start to want to be something good, to do something redeemable that makes people proud …*

I flipped the lights off and crawled under the sheets with Chris's ashes, wishing I had more vodka or rum. *I'd even settle for a Jell-O shot.*

Chapter 12

It was barely eight o'clock in the morning, but Whole Spring's lobby was already full of patients. I signed in at the front desk and asked to speak with Aaron. The bartender hadn't given me his last name, so my fingers were crossed there wasn't more than one Aaron employed here.

I'd stopped by the *Manger*'s office this morning and paid him a hundred dollars. I'd expected him to ask questions—about Valerie, or how long I planned to stay—but he'd swiped the money and that was it.

The lady working the counter at Whole Spring was behind a Plexiglass wall, and I couldn't help feeling like a criminal as she wearily instructed me to take a seat. "I'll let him know you're here," she said.

A man wearing glasses and too-high suspenders sat beside me. His lips were moving, some silent dialogue only he could hear.

After thirty minutes, I was starting to wonder if this was a mistake ... but then a wooden door in the wall swung open and a guy with spiky brown hair and fashionably ripped jeans called my name.

"Do we have an appointment today?" He didn't look suspicious of me, just curious.

"No, but I was hoping you could help me," I said, tucking my hands in my pockets. My clothes were rank; I hadn't changed them in a couple days.

"I'm looking for a friend of mine and I think you know her. Valerie from Rook Pharmaceuticals," I said, quietly. I could feel people watching us in the lobby. I shifted from foot to foot, hoping for a more private place to ask him questions.

"Ah, okay. Why don't you follow me?" Aaron said. I did just that, zigzagging through windy corridors filled with doors, some open and some closed. I could hear quiet voices behind them, people talking in their therapy sessions. I tried to imagine the secrets that were shared between these featureless walls ...

"This is me," Aaron said, pointing to a small eight-by-eight room with no windows inside it. There was a desk and two soft leather chairs, but the office was cramped and devoid of artwork. I did notice a neatly framed diploma on the wall behind Aaron's desk—*Aaron Andes, L.C.S.W.*

Aaron took a seat behind the desk and I plopped into one of the chairs, adjusting my hair around my face even though it did very little to hide my scars.

Lincoln's words came floating back to me ... *Did he really say I was beautiful? I definitely don't feel beautiful ...*

Aaron examined my face, his expression kind but thoughtful.

"Do you know Valerie Hutchens?" I asked, getting straight to the point.

"I do." He folded his hands on the desk in front of him, then steepled his fingers—*I wonder if he practiced this therapy stance in grad school.*

I waited for him to elaborate, to tell me how he knew her, but the silence continued.

"I talked to the bartender at *Cavern* last night ... he said Valerie was meeting with you and some other people that work here. Maybe trying to sell some new samples from Rook, I presume? You see, the problem is ... she asked me to come here and now I can't find her."

Aaron didn't react the way I'd expected him to. He got up, closed the door to his office, then sat back down. His expression was strangely neutral.

Finally, he said, "I've known Valerie for years, ever since she got in the industry. We are acquaintances, I guess you could say. I'd call us friends. She talked a lot about her aunt and mentioned a few friends back in Wisconsin ... but I don't think I know you. What did you say your name was again?"

There's the suspicion I was waiting for.

"Camilla," I said, conveniently leaving out my last name in case he decided to look me up and discovered my recent ash-stealing scandal. "Valerie and I went to middle and high school together. Truth is, I'm worried about her. I was hoping

148

you might know where she went ... you said you know her, right? Do you know how to get in contact with her besides social media? She stopped responding to my messages ..."

Aaron shook his head. "I don't. I used to have her number, but I don't think I do anymore. To be honest, I'm a little worried about her too."

A rush of relief washed over me. *Finally, someone else is concerned. Not just me.*

He continued: "Valerie posts constantly on social media ... I'm not sure if you follow her ...?"

I nodded, probably a little too enthusiastically.

"She hasn't posted anything since she quit. I'm just hoping she's in a good headspace and didn't do anything too hasty."

I raised my eyebrows. "I do follow her accounts, and that's exactly why I'm worried. It's like she fell off the face of the earth. But what do you mean by 'quit'?"

Aaron raised his eyebrows, his first real noticeable emotion. "Oh. Well, she was quitting the industry. Said she didn't like pushing pills anymore. She put in her notice last week."

Now it was my turn to look surprised. "Really? That's odd, considering she was just talking about going to New Orleans on business ..."

"Right." Aaron steepled his fingers again, his eyes boring into mine so intensely that I felt like I was being examined by an X-ray machine. *It's a good thing you can't see inside my soul, Aaron. It's dark as shit in here.*

"She met with you and your colleagues on business. Why would she do that if she was quitting her job at Rook?" I kept pushing.

Aaron nodded. "Well, initially, we assumed it was business. We all love Valerie. She lights up the entire office when she walks inside it. I hadn't seen her come through Paducah in nearly a year, so I was eager to meet with her. We all were. But she dropped a bombshell on us ... told us that she was leaving the biz and wanted to say goodbye."

He's lying. My mind floated back to that post on Instagram. **#allworknoplay #hustling.**

But why *is he lying to me? That's the real question ...*

"It's just hard for me to believe."

Aaron's face turned serious again. "How do you know Valerie? You told me your name and that you went to school with her, but not how you're connected to her now ... Do you work in the pharmaceutical industry?"

I cleared my throat. "No, I don't. We're just friends. I'm concerned, that's all ..."

"I see. Well, Valerie didn't like the job, but that's not the only reason she was quitting ... She had a stalker. Someone was following her."

"I know!" I said, a little too loudly. Excited to have someone who agreed with me on something, I dug my phone out of my pocket and held up the photo of the man at the concert. "Do you recognize this man? I've seen him in the background of a few of her photos. He might be the one ..."

Aaron stared at the picture, his jaw flexing for a split second. "I don't know him. I really only knew Valerie professionally. But I was worried when she mentioned the stalker."

I flipped my phone shut. "Here's the thing ... I haven't seen Valerie in years. I know it seems odd, but we're friends online and I don't know how to reach her ..."

"You're not her stalker, are you?" Aaron smiled, but it didn't reach his eyes. *He is serious.*

I could feel my face growing warmer, probably turning the shade of a Fuji apple ...

"Certainly not," I breathed.

"Well, I don't know where she went, and I haven't talked to her. I told you all that I know. If she's your friend, why don't you have her number?"

He was back in his therapist's stance. His eyes traveled the road map of scars on my face, then down to the frayed edges of my sweatshirt. *I fought the urge to do a breath-check—can he smell the alcohol on me?*

"Well, we mostly just chat online, that's why," I said, voice barely above a whisper.

He really thinks I might be the stalker, I realized, in horror.

"Well, thanks for your help, Aaron. I appreciate you talking to me."

Moments later, he was leading me back down the hall. Suddenly, it felt narrower, with less air to breathe. I was so embarrassed that I had to get out of there fast.

"Thanks," I mumbled for the second time, parting

ways with him in the lobby. I nodded at the man in the suspenders. He was still talking to himself, and when I nodded, he shot me a jolted, paranoid look, like I was a Russian spy giving out some sort of signal.

I need to get the hell out of this place, now!

Outside, snowflakes were falling again, like little diamond flecks in the sky. I stuck my tongue out as I walked back to the truck, feeling childish, and still reeling from Aaron's suggestion that *I* was the stalker.

So, Valerie quit her job. Maybe she left and gave up her social media because of it. Maybe she went off the grid for her own safety. But where is she now?

I imagined the lonely drive back to Wisconsin ... and the hellish consequences lying in wait for me when I got there.

I stuck my key in the ignition and turned it. Nothing happened.

Again, and again, I tried to start the truck.

"Dammit."

I climbed back out, icy-cold wind blasting me in the face, my hair flying around wildly and getting stuck in the corners of my mouth.

The library was only two blocks away. If I could get there, I could find Lincoln and contact a tow truck.

Lincoln's eyes widened in surprise when I strolled up to the counter.

"Truck's dead," I said, teeth chattering uncontrollably from the cold.

"Oh. I'm sorry to hear that. I can give you a lift when I get off ...?"

"Not necessary. I'm going to have to get it towed to the closest mechanic, I guess."

Lincoln shook his head. "Don't do that. I'm good with my hands. I might be able to fix it and save you some money." I looked at his smooth, white hands as they softly glided library slips full of patrons' names into the back of the library books. I couldn't imagine those hands working on cars, but I also couldn't imagine them holding a gun or fighting a war ...

"Okay. But I still need to get online if that's okay ... What time do you get off?"

"Three. Grab any open computer you want."

They were all open, so I chose the one up against the farthest wall in the children's book section. My stomach grumbled noisily as I pulled up Valerie's pages to check for updates. *I need food and a good night's sleep, but not as much as I need to find out where Valerie is ...*

Maybe she's fine ... maybe this whole trip was pointless. Hell, maybe I made this trip just as an excuse to get away from Oshkosh ...

My hands shook as I realized there was a new message from Valerie in my inbox.

There were no words, just a picture. Majestic mountains dotted with lush green, red, and orange vegetation filled the screen. A blanket of fog hovered above the ridges, so smoky it blocked out the sky.

What the hell?

I'd never been to Tennessee, but I had no doubt—these were the Smoky Mountains.

Where are you? I'm looking for you in Paducah, I messaged.

I didn't expect a response from her, but moments later, she'd written back.

I'm sorry, I'm in Gatlinburg now.

Gatlinburg? Was Valerie messing with me? Now there was only one thing left to do: go home.

Disappointed, I wrote back: **Have fun.**

What else could I say?

It was time to go home and face the music.

Beg Chris's mom to drop the charges so I won't go to jail. The thought of begging Bonnie Brown for anything made my stomach curl in disgust.

"Judy's going to take over. I can drive you to your truck now." I startled in my seat as I realized Lincoln was standing behind me. I closed out Valerie's page and smiled awkwardly up at him.

"Okay, great. I'm ready to go."

Side by side, we walked out of the library. I was overcome with melancholy, and regret. *Why did I steal the ashes in the first place? And why did I come here, searching for a girl who barely knows I'm alive? How could I be this fucking stupid? This fucking impulsive …*

"Hey." Lincoln nudged me. "Where'd you go? You look like you're a million miles away."

I shrugged, letting him open the door of his Jeep for me. The powdery white flakes were gone, replaced by warm sunshine that had no place in my life. *I want the storms to return ... that would be more fitting for my black mood.*

"Just a lot on my mind," I said, climbing in and securing my seatbelt. We rode in silence, back to my truck. When we got there, I stood outside, shivering, while Lincoln bent over the hood.

He looked good, in corduroy pants and a soft, black sweater. I watched the material of his shirt slide up, revealing two dimples on his lower back.

"I think it needs a new transmission." He stood up and grimaced, then wiped his palms on the sides of his pants.

"Fuck." I pressed my forehead against the driver's-side window of the truck, wishing I'd never come here in the first place.

It took hours for the tow truck to show up, but I was thankful to have Lincoln waiting with me. While we waited, I filled him in on my meeting with Aaron, and Valerie's message that she was in Gatlinburg.

"I wish she'd told you she was okay and saved you the trip. Why would she ask you to come, then leave? That's pretty shady," Lincoln said, gnawing on his nail beds. His hands were so clean, his fingernails shaped like perfect half-moons. I thought about Chris, the way he used to chew his nails down to the nubs and it annoyed the shit out of me ... *Oh what I wouldn't give to watch him do that now.*

"Truth is, I haven't seen Valerie in over a decade."

"Come again?" Lincoln said, snorting with laughter. I couldn't help it; his laugh was infectious, and I felt myself giggling, too. *It is so ridiculous, when I hear myself say it out loud.*

"It's silly, I know. I haven't seen her since high school. But here I am ... tracking down a stranger from the internet simply because she said she needed my help."

Lincoln considered that, tilting his head left to right in thought. "You know ... it's pretty sweet, actually. Nowadays, people are so absorbed in their own lives. It's kind of refreshing, really. I would kill for a friend like that."

"You would?" I laughed again, but his face was serious.

"I would. She's lucky to have you as a friend, even if she doesn't know it, Camilla."

"Thank you." I felt a jittery feeling in my stomach and a warmness in my chest. *Acceptance, this must be what it feels like.*

Talking came easily with Lincoln. He talked a bit about his time in the service. He'd joined the army because he didn't want to go to college after high school. "I didn't realize what I'd gotten myself into," he admitted.

"And how did you become a librarian? Soldier to librarian, it just doesn't seem very ... I don't know, normal?"

He choked with laughter. "I didn't know what I wanted to study. The army paid for my undergrad degree, but nothing appealed to me ... The one thing I always loved was books. And I can't write for shit. So, what else was there? I just wanted to do something that put me close to books, if that makes sense ..."

"It does," I said, a pang in my chest as I thought about my own writing, abandoned years ago ...

"Most of my friends went into the police force when they got back. They tried to pressure me into joining the academy, but I would have made a terrible cop. It helps, though, having cops as friends, I guess."

"You'd be good at anything you did. You're a man who laughs like a girl and opens car doors like an old man and loves books like a saint ... where the hell did you come from, Lincoln Smalls?"

For a moment, as he laughed and teased me back, I felt guilty again. *I'm flirting ... how and why am I flirting with this man?*

Lincoln's phone chimed on the table between us, the moment gone. "That's the library," he said, shaking his head. "I have to go help Judy find a missing book."

"Good luck with that. Do you mind dropping me back off at the motel first?"

"Sure thing," Lincoln said.

My feelings were all over the place on the way to *The Rest EZ*. Ashamed about my misguided hunt for Valerie, confused by my attraction to Lincoln, anxious about what awaited me at home ...

I was relieved to get back inside the motel and pop my last few remaining pills.

My head instantly hazy, I flipped the TV on and climbed into bed. *I might just have to pay the "manger" for a few more days … anything to escape going home just yet,* I considered. I had no idea how long it would take to fix the truck, but I hoped not very long. *What if it's a major problem and it can't be fixed at all?* I lamented.

I stared at the local Paducah news station, my head buzzy and warm. A "breaking news" report came scrolling across the bottom of the screen.

"Everything is breaking news these days," I groaned, grabbing for the remote. I turned the TV back off, then rolled onto my side. My gaze was immediately drawn to the window. The glare from my bedside lamp cast a reflection on the window; I couldn't see outside, only my own image lying in bed echoing back at me.

I turned onto my other side, staring at the sad, empty desk along the wall.

What are you running from, Valerie? Why would you give up your job and go somewhere like Gatlinburg, Tennessee? I hadn't been to Gatlinburg before, but I had this idea in my head of what it looked like—Christmas-y decorations all year round and cheesy, overpriced tourist attractions, Dollywood …

As I stared at the desk, imagining Valerie perched in the clunky chair that went with it, I was hit with a prickling sensation. As though I were being watched …

I couldn't shake off the unnerving feeling of isolation here in Paducah—my sister was hundreds of miles away, my truck was in a shop across town ... if someone wanted to get me, now would be the perfect time to do it.

I pinched my eyes shut, fighting off the urge to call or text Lincoln. *I don't know him; he doesn't know me. It's stupid to trust him. And it's stupid of him to trust me ...*

But there was something between us—a spark—I'd felt it that first day, and I'd felt it again today. Still ... I didn't know him very well. It was silly to call him because I was scared.

I tossed and turned for an hour, finally turning on the TV set again just for noise. In this dumpy motel, I was surprised that they'd invested in smart TVs, but then again, I wasn't. *We can't survive without our entertainment, can we?*

I turned on Netflix, straining to recall my username and password that I used at home. It had been so long since I'd watched anything. But when the black-and-red screen loaded, I was surprised to see an unfamiliar avatar already displayed on the main page.

A cartoon character, with bright-pink hair and shiny-blue eyes, the name "Val" beneath it.

Valerie must have forgotten to log out of Netflix before she left.

I clicked on her avatar, a satisfying feeling washing over me, as though I were catching an unseen glimpse into Valerie's head. I was slightly disappointed as I scanned through her "Continue Watching" picks—she was a fan of reality TV and young-adult dramas.

Oh well. I guess she's as bored and lonely as I am. There was never anything good on to watch anyway. I propped the pillows up behind my head and stretched out with the remote in my hand. I clicked on season one of *Gossip Girl*, hoping I'd fall asleep.

Two hours in, I was still restless. Resolutely, I got out of bed and stretched my legs. Soundlessly, I slipped on my last pair of clean pants—stretchy rainbow-colored yoga pants that used to belong to Hannah—and stuffed my feet inside my boots without socks, and without tying them.

I couldn't sleep until I checked out the other side of that window. I just couldn't shake the feeling that the stalker was back there behind the building, prowling through the shadows, peeking inside …

Adrenaline surged through my veins as I cupped my key card in my hand and opened the door to my motel room. I was met with a blast of cool air and something fluttering in my ear … *a moth flying around on a snowy day?*

I stepped outside in the dark. My hands were shaking as I lit a cigarette.

I flipped on my flashlight app, grateful for what little light it emitted from the screen.

Tentatively, I scanned the concrete patio that connected all the rooms. No one else was outside. There were only three cars sitting quietly in the parking lot. A cloud of low-settling fog seeped over the entire lot and building.

"Fuck it," I said, puffing on my cigarette as I slid around the side of the building. The grass was overgrown and itchy around my ankles as I followed the windowless brick wall to the backside of the building. The ground was marshy and cold, my boots digging in with every step, encasing them in icy mud.

As I rounded the backside of the building, I was relieved to see no one hiding there outside my window. *Did I really expect there would be?*

Maybe.

On the other side of my motel window, I was just tall enough—if I stood on my tiptoes—to look inside my own room. The curtains were drawn, but sheer, and sure enough, I had a dimly lit view of my bed and the desk where Valerie had been sitting. I could see the glow of the TV screen casting greenish shadows around the room. Blair Waldorf was planning something vindictive again.

For a moment, I could see Valerie there, clear as day, slouched on the bed watching *Gossip Girl*, her perfectly painted toenails pointed up at the ceiling as she sipped her Vitamin Water and relaxed ...

"What on earth are you doing out here?"

"Jesus!" I jumped back from the window, my right foot sliding on a slippery patch of wet grass. I caught myself, scraping my hand on the brick wall and feeling like I'd pulled a muscle in my crotch as I regained my balance.

"You scared the hell out of me," I stammered, staring at the building manager. He was gripping two plastic bags of garbage in his left hand. It was then that I noticed a large metal dumpster against the back of the building, between the backside of rooms 11 and 10. I hadn't been able to see it from my window the first time I looked ...

"Just tossing out my garbage," he said, shaking the bags at me as proof.

He wandered over to the large dumpster, tossed the bags inside, and slammed the lid down so hard, I jumped. *He must have come around the other side of the building. I didn't even hear him,* I realized.

"You always take out the garbage this late?"

His lips spread, widening into a mischievous smile. "No, not really. It's just ... I had company tonight. A woman."

"Ah," I said, not sure if I believed him.

He glanced at the window, then looked back at me, waiting for an explanation of why I was outside creeping around this late at night. I felt strangely caught in the act of a crime as he strolled over to me, casually swinging his short, chubby arms. He stopped right beside me, edging up on the tips of his toes to look in my room.

"What ya peering into your own room for?" He was close, *too close*, out here in the dark. I could smell the booze on his breath mixed with the pungent aroma of body odor. *Was he outside my room looking in earlier? Was it his eyes I sensed through the curtains?* I shook my head. *I'm just being paranoid.*

I'd seen the man looking in at Valerie, and he looked nothing like this creep.

"What are you doing?" he asked me again, talking slowly as though I was hard of hearing.

"You can see right into my room. I felt like someone

was out here, watching me or something ... I needed to check before I went to sleep."

He snorted. "No one hanging out back here, I promise. These woods go far back, forty acres, and then they connect to a highway ... we only have one other guest staying here, so unless it was her or me carrying out garbage, no one was back here."

"Where did all those old rides come from ...?"

"Ah. They belonged to my dad. Before the motel here was built, these grounds were used for the 4-H fair. I tried to sell them years ago but didn't get any takers. And as you can see, they're too rusty and old to sell now. I guess I could scrap them for metal or something ... but getting someone to come pick that heavy shit up ... near impossible, ya know?"

I nodded, wishing I hadn't asked. I needed another cigarette.

"Want me to install some new blinds for you tomorrow?"

Surprised by his offer, I said, "Yes, please. I would really appreciate that."

"Well, good night to ya then," he said, scratching his beard and wandering back across the field to the other side of the building, walking bow-legged.

I watched him go and was just about to turn around and head inside myself, when he stopped and looked back at me again.

"Oh yeah, I almost forgot. Cops were here today, asking about that friend of yours."

"Come again?" My breath froze in my chest.

"Yeah," he said, still scratching his beard, "I guess you was right about her going missing. Only, from what it sounds like on the news, they're less worried about her and more worried about her dead auntie."

Dead auntie.

"Her aunt died? What happened ...?"

He tucked his hands in his pockets and rocked forward and back on the balls of his feet, as though he was nervous about something.

"Uhhh ... the cops said she was murdered. They're trying to track down Valerie and make sure she's safe, and not involved."

The thought of police officers scrounging around the motel made me sick.

Valerie's Aunt Janet was dead ...

This is too much to wrap my brain around right now.

Oh Valerie, you must be so sad and so scared ...

"How was she murdered?" I asked, barely breathing.

Janet was just commenting on Valerie's posts a couple days ago ... how could she be dead? Why would someone kill her? Could it have been Valerie's supposed stalker?

"Stabbed to death. One cop mentioned something like forty-two knife wounds ... that's brutal, man. I guess now they want to talk to your friend but she's in the wind."

Hopefully, she hasn't been taken hostage by the same person who killed her aunt, I thought, grimly.

"Did you give them any info about the guy who checked her out of the motel? That probably would have been helpful," I said, suddenly annoyed by this man. His stance of complete privacy wasn't doing Valerie any favors ...

"I did, but he could have been anyone ... her boyfriend, even."

"What did he look like?" I asked, thinking again about the man in the photos.

"He looked like any Tom, Dick, and Harry off the street. Sandy-colored hair, strong jaw. Like I said, it wasn't the guy in the photo you showed me. But I do hope your friend is okay. She seemed ... sweet."

"I hope so, too," I said, still reeling. I couldn't imagine what Valerie was thinking right now—*Does she know what happened to her Aunt Janet, is that why she rushed out of town? Or ... did someone force her to leave?*

"I'm Bruce, by the way," he said, giving me a little wave before walking off.

I was gasping for air when I got back inside my room. I was craving more pills and a stiff drink to soothe me.

I scooped up my bottles, but then, remembering they were empty, I threw them across the room. I waited for the scream to burst out of me ... but it was bottled up tight.

Why would someone kill Janet ... and who? I wondered.

Maybe Valerie didn't go to Gatlinburg by choice ... Is she running from something, or was she taken?

Chapter 13

The misspelled *"Manger"* sign was hanging by a single strip of duct tape. The wind bristled, flipping it upside down, just as the door flew open. Bruce's thinning hair was disheveled, his eyes crusted in the corners with sleep.

He wobbled on his feet, struggling to tuck his half-open shirt into a pair of worn-out Levi's. His feet were bare, yellowish-brown toenails jutting out from each toe.

He saw me looking down at his feet and cursed.

"Long night," he said, clearing his throat.

Last night, he'd claimed to have company ... but the office behind him looked empty.

"Ah. Well, good for you," I said, awkwardly. "Sorry to bother you, but I wanted to see about those blinds ..."

His eyebrows crinkled. *Surely, he hasn't forgotten already.*

"My room, remember? You offered to put up some blinds when we talked last night ..."

"Oh, yeah! Of course. Let me grab my shoes and keys. I keep most of my spare stuff for the rooms next door."

I followed him inside and listened as he stumbled

around in the back room of his office, looking wildly for his shoes. I took a seat on the dingy loveseat, then laid my head back and closed my eyes.

When he came back out, keys rattling in his hand, my eyes remained closed.

"Ya ready?" he asked, the question laced with mild irritation.

"Is it okay if I wait here for you? I'm having the worst menstrual cramps today."

He groaned, clearly disgusted.

"I guess that would be alright. Be back in a second."

I massaged my temples as I waited for him to leave. He didn't close the door all the way, merely left it ajar.

Damn. For my sake, I hope he's gone for more than a "second".

As soon as he was gone, I popped up from the seat, heart racing, and scurried behind his desk. Immediately, I checked the two deep metal drawers on either side of the desk. They were filled with thin manila folders. I knew this was where he kept his guest information because I'd seen him take out a file and replace it when I checked in.

There were hundreds of files, and as I quickly browsed through them, I realized they weren't in any particular order. *Dammit.*

I flipped through a few. There were guest numbers and signatures but trying to find the one filled out by Valerie would be like looking for a four-leaf clover in an overgrown field. There were banging sounds next door; clearly, I needed more time to go through these files.

Gently, I closed the left and right drawers, then tiptoed over to the window beside his desk. It was the same size as the one inside my motel room. It also had sheer curtains barely covering the pane. I unlocked the two bolts at the top and scurried back to my spot on the loveseat.

When Bruce returned moments later, I was still massaging my temples.

"Here's your blinds. I guess I'll follow you over to your room and hang them up for ya. If you're feeling well enough to leave now …?"

I jumped up. "Thank you, I'm so much better now! No need for you to come. I can hang them up on my own."

"Well, okay, if you're sure?"

"I'm sure." I scooped the heavy blinds from his arms, grunting under the weight of them.

I didn't know when I'd have a chance to slip in through the window to his office, but as soon as the moment struck, I was going to dig into those files.

Bruce wasn't lying about the woman. She was busty and tall, with wild, canary-blonde hair, and an ear-splitting laugh that rang out across the parking lot and reverberated all the way down the walkway to room 14. The air was noticeably warmer today, the stinging chill from last night all but evaporated. I puffed on my Pall Mall, pretending not to watch the two lovebirds. They were standing outside the office, so caught up in their embrace that they hadn't noticed me watching. Their kisses were sloppy—sickening, really—and every few seconds, the woman came up for air, that high-pitched giggle ringing like a broken doorbell in my head. I willed them to go into Bruce's room, but moments later, they were stumbling inside the *Manger*'s office again.

Fuck.

I stubbed my cigarette out, trying to formulate a secondary plan of action. I couldn't get in that room until Bruce's fat ass came out of it. And he'd been inside all day with her, the yellow canary.

I was just about to go back to my room and admit defeat, when the laugh returned. I watched them stumble out the door of his office, a tangled ball of drunken desire, a bottle of what looked like gin in her hand, and they stopped in front of the room next door to the office. Bruce jammed a key into the lock while she groped his saggy ass from behind.

Finally, they stumbled inside his room, and it was my time to act. I slithered around the back of the building.

Quietly, I traipsed past the rusty old rides and the other rooms. I had to bypass Bruce's room on my way to his office, and somehow quietly sneak in the office window without him seeing or hearing me do it ...

As I approached room 2, I was relieved to find thick venetian blinds covering the window completely. Apparently, Bruce valued his own privacy more than his guests'.

Not only did I not want to catch a glimpse of him and the giggle-queen fucking, but I didn't want him to see me, creeping outside his window like a freakish stalker.

169

I winced, Aaron's accusation floating back to me. *Maybe I am a stalker. Who goes to this much trouble for someone they barely know?*

But I remembered that moment in the bathroom stall ... Valerie had *needed* me, she'd been so upset ... and now she was begging me, pleading me to come help her ...

I'm trying to get to you, Valerie.

For my sake, I hoped Bruce's chronic drunkenness made him a slow performer in bed. I needed time to go through those files.

I'd considered another option—stealing the files and taking them back to my room—*but there's no way I could carry all of them, even if I didn't get caught, and who's to say I'd grab the right ones, anyway?*

Pressing my back against the wall between Bruce's window and the office window, I closed my eyes and took a deep breath. I could hear laughter and movement coming from inside his room, and the crooning of country music playing in the background.

This might be my only chance.

I counted to three, then I faced the office window. I put my hands on the ledge, and lifted, hoping Bruce hadn't spotted the disengaged lock and re-locked it since my earlier visit.

The window glided up easily and I let out a deep whoosh of breath.

The ledge was higher than I'd anticipated, and I groaned with pain as I lifted myself up and swung one leg over the sill. For a moment, I hesitated, hanging there, half in and half out the window, worrying they might have heard me ... but then I realized I could still hear the woman's cacophonous laughter and Garth Brooks singing his heart out.

Painfully, I tugged my other leg over and fell with a thump on the carpet inside. I sat for a few seconds, catching my breath, then I quietly pulled myself up to my feet and slid the window closed behind me.

The office itself was dark, but the afternoon sun provided natural light to read by. I opened both file drawers and tried to scan the names as fast as possible. It took several long minutes to figure out, but there was a method to Bruce's madness. Instead of organizing the guests' names alphabetically, he'd sorted their files by dates of occupancy, as though he pulled the file out and stuck the most recent one in the front each time someone checked in or out.

I was easily able to rule out the drawer on the right—it had the oldest files, dating back all the way to 2015. I closed that one, focusing on the left drawer.

I started with my own file in the front, then flipped back, scanning the dates and names. Less than a dozen guests had checked into *The Rest EZ* over the last two weeks. As I scanned the generic form, I realized that there was a space for their name and date of check-in/check-out, and a blank space for room numbers. The forms were skeletal at best, providing very little useful info. But still, I needed to see Valerie's. Needed to make sure there wasn't any info Bruce was leaving out.

I kept flipping, scanning the room numbers, and stopping only when I saw "14". As I skipped past other guest forms, I realized that Bruce had written notes on some of them. "Has a thing for hookers." "Sells blow." "Hot piece of ass."

Disgusting.

And that's when I saw it: Valerie Hutchens' name, scrawled across the top of a guest form from October 2nd. I left the file but removed the sheet, then folded it into a tiny, neat square. I shoved the square into my back pocket and shut the drawer up tight.

Muffled moans from next door came seeping through the vent that connected the rooms. My stomach curled in on itself.

With the paper in my pocket, I had what I'd come for. But just for good measure, I slid open the thin top drawer in the desk. As suspected, it was lined with pencils and pens, but there was something else there, too. I scooped up two small bottles of Jim Beam.

Carefully, I eased myself back out the window and slid it back into place. This time, I ran past Bruce's room, panting all the way to room 14. I could already feel the whiskey burning in my veins.

Valerie had checked into *The Rest EZ* at 5:00 on the evening of October 2nd. She paid for a week-long stay, in cash. I scanned down, struggling to read Bruce's chicken-scratch notes. *"Red Miata. Pretty girl. BF comes late at night."*

My skin crawled. *Was the stalker coming at night while she slept, spying on her?* I remembered that midnight video, when she said a man had followed her home from the club. *Why would she choose to walk along those poorly lit, broken sidewalks to meet up with Aaron and his co-workers at Cavern?*

But I knew the answer to that. She probably went to the bar on foot, so she wouldn't have to drink and drive. There were many times I'd drunk too much and should have walked instead.

Wish I'd have been that smart and responsible. Maybe if I had, Chris wouldn't be dead.

At the bottom of the form, Bruce had written: *"Room 14 – checked out Oct 10. Paid in full by Chris, cash."*

But the rest of the sentence was blurry—because my eyes were zeroed in on one word and one word only: *Chris.*

It was ridiculous, an absurd coincidence ... *After all, the name Chris is probably the most common, following John, James, Paul, and David ...*

I twisted the caps off both the whiskeys and drained them, my eyes never leaving the page ...

Chapter 14

There's a pool of red-rose blood in my mouth. I could spit it out if I wanted to, but I also need to taste it. I need to taste the pain that I caused ... force myself to endure the bitter, coppery brine. After all, I'm the reason he's bleeding. I can't lift my arms or move my legs, it's like my entire body is composed of doll parts. Stiff and plastic and dead. It reminds me of another time I couldn't feel my limbs ... the time Chris got mad, a little too rough in the bedroom ...

Psst. I'm back here, ya know ... The voice is familiar, younger than Chris's voice. My arm flops like a cooked spaghetti noodle, my fingertips teasing the edge of the rearview mirror, trying to match a face to the voice. I tip the mirror, just enough to bump it up a notch.

Her eyes are round like quarters, her wavy hair golden in the flicker of emergency lights. There are rosy-red strips of blood in her hair.

I'm right here. I've been back here all along, she tells me. Fifteen-year-old Valerie Hutchens is in the backseat of the Buick. It's not just her head—*thank god, she's more than a head*—but in her lap there's a present. *Don't,* I whisper. Chris's blood drips from my mouth and onto my chin. *Don't,* I beg through bloody lips. The shiny blue gift-wrapping falls away like feathers, exposing what's hidden inside.

Chris's nose and mouth ... the scar on his brow ... are peeking out through the paper. *Surprise,* she says. She smiles, the corners of her lips turning up so high they threaten to split and tear ...

My arms are numb as I realize I'm dreaming again. I keep my eyes pinched shut.

I can feel him between the sheets.

The knotty curve of his spine. The soft bits of fuzz on his shoulders. The mole above his tailbone. The tension in his back and shoulders; always a part of him that was angry, like me ...

I run my knuckles over his back bones. *Press harder,* he says. *Dig in.*

When I opened my eyes, I was alone in my motel room. My stomach did a somersault, the events from the day before gushing back like a tidal wave.

I'm in over my head—I have no idea how to help Valerie at this point.

Her aunt is dead. Murdered. And Valerie's missing—but is she gone by choice or by force? I do not know. Again, she's not answering me ...

And a man named Chris, who looks like my Chris, could be the one who took her.

Rationally, I know it's not him—my Chris is as dead as a doornail—but maybe there's a small part of me, the part losing control, that wishes that in some other life, some alternate universe, he is there ...

Shoving the blankets and sheets aside, I stared at the clock on the nightstand. The smudgy red numbers blinked back at me.

My head throbbed from the whiskey, and withdrawals from the pills. *I need something ... something to keep me going ...*

I could have gone back to sleep. But there was no way I was taking the chance of getting sucked back into that dream. *No fucking way.*

I paced the floor of Jimmy's garage while Lincoln sat slumped comfortably in a chair in the waiting room. He looked so relaxed and calm that it was borderline annoying.

"Jimmy said it'd take a while longer. We don't have to wait here, Camilla. He'll call us when it's done ..."

I stopped pacing, staring at the closed door, listening for Jimmy working on my truck on the other side.

The lobby smelled like diesel and floor wax; the plastic waiting chairs so stiff they were making my back ache. Pacing felt good; I needed to burn off this excess energy.

"You sure you're okay?" Lincoln asked.

"Yeah, just didn't sleep much last night."

Lincoln knew I was searching for my friend, but he had no idea who she was ... I was hesitant to mention her full name in case he came across a news report about her murdered aunt.

"Why are you in such a hurry to get back home? If you want me to take you to look for your friend, I will ..."

"Thanks, Lincoln. I appreciate all your help, really, I do. I need to get back home to Wisconsin."

"I understand ..." But I could hear the disappointment in his voice.

A half hour later, we were still waiting. The door to the garage stayed closed, tools clanking loudly behind it, the only sound that reassured me it was getting done.

Lincoln offered to go pick up some sandwiches for us, and I was relieved to catch a break from him. I liked him—maybe I liked him a little too much, honestly—but I could tell he sensed my unease, that he knew something was wrong ... and if he asked me a few more times, I'd probably wind up telling him the whole truth about Valerie.

Confusion lingered, my emotions over Valerie playing tug-of-war inside me.

Nothing about this made sense or jived with Valerie's character. *Could she be involved in her aunt's murder? No freaking way.*

But what do I really know about Valerie? I only see what she wants me to see ... what she allows all of us to see on social media. And a public persona is often different than reality ...

177

I took my phone out, staring so hard at my empty contact list that my eyes watered from exhaustion. I needed sleep.

Everything is getting that hazy look around the edges to it … and I'm officially out of my medication, and the withdrawals will get worse before they get better …

I needed to unblock my sister and give her a call. Before I went home, I had to assess the situation and Hannah could be my gauge. But instead of unblocking her, I looked up Bonnie Brown on Facebook.

We weren't friends—never had been—which made sense considering we were never friends in real life. *If I can say one good thing about Bonnie: at least she's honest. Besides that first day we met, she's never bothered pretending that she likes me. It's been blatantly obvious all along that she doesn't.*

Some of Bonnie's profile pics and posts were public, and occasionally, I liked to see what she was up to—at least I used to, when Chris was still alive.

I hadn't checked her page in a while, and honestly, I was scared to.

Her profile pic looked as it had for a while—a snapshot of her and Chris, their warm brown eyes and jet-black hair made them almost look like twins.

I sighed, staring at Chris's face and neck … and his shoulders and chest. I wanted my husband back, and in one piece … he was so handsome in this photo, so solid and so *alive* …

I scrolled down to look at Bonnie's page, my eyes

instantly locking in on a public post at the very top of her profile. I stared at the words, my mouth falling open in horror.

My ex-daughter-in-law not only stole my dear son's ashes (THE SON SHE KILLED!) but she also took my great-grandad's water pot and stole a 9mm handgun from my room (a present from my DEAD SON!). Please keep an eye out for that crazy bitch. She is a danger to society! Call the police if you see her. CALL THE POLICE, PLEASE.

223 people like this post.

"Thanks," I said, accepting a sandwich and an extra-large Polar Pop from Lincoln.

"Turkey and cheese okay?"

"It's fine," I said, already stuffing a bite of it into my mouth. The gas-station sandwich was part soggy, part stale, but I was ravenous, eating so fast I could barely finish swallowing the final bite. I guzzled down the soda, feeling a jolt as the caffeine hit my bloodstream. My hands were shaking badly ... caffeine wasn't going to cut it. *I need my pills. I need a drink.*

Lincoln was watching me, his eyes creased with concern.

"Everything okay?"

If he asks me that one more time, I might snap his neck.

I nodded, taking another big gulp of soda. I set the pop on the floor by my feet. "Just eager to get home, I guess." I imagined what my homecoming would be like—the local

179

Oshkosh police, all two of them, snapping cuffs around my wrists.

I can't go back there again.

Lincoln smiled that sorrowful half-smile, making me wonder why he cared so much that I was leaving ...

The door to the garage swung open and a rough-looking man barreled through it, fingers tucked into thick loops on his stained-up carpenter jeans. He had a long white beard and too many tattoos to count. He introduced himself as Jimmy.

Maybe he has a local connection and can get me some Lortabs and Xanax, I considered, eyeing his biker tattoos.

"You're ready to go," he smiled, dangling out the keys to my truck like a gift. They *were* a gift; I never thought I'd be so grateful to have that rusty old truck back again, but I was.

I paid the painful price of 2700 dollars, wincing as I accepted the receipt. At this rate, I'd be broke in a couple weeks ... *but maybe I won't need any money, considering I might be in jail soon.*

I imagined the look of sheer satisfaction on Bonnie's face as the doors to my jail cell slammed shut. I'd finally get what was coming to me—*after all, that's what they all want, right?*

Maybe the weight of my mistakes is strapped to me, like a bowling ball to my chest, and they're pulling me down down down all on their own, no choice left in the matter ...

"Thanks again for being such a huge help," I said to

Lincoln as we stood next to my truck in the parking lot. "It's been nice getting to know you. And ... thank you for your service to our country. I never told you that, even though you told me you were army ..."

I stuck out my hand, but Lincoln pushed it away and reached in for a hug.

There was static electricity between us, heat emanating from his chest and warming up mine. As I gripped him in a hug, I held on tight for a second, hands grazing over the bulging muscles in his shoulders and back. *How long has it been since I touched a man?*

"Will you call me sometime?" Lincoln asked, his expression adorably hopeful as we pulled apart.

"Definitely," I promised, climbing into the truck and slamming the door. As much as I liked him, my thoughts were on my next move ... and right now, that involved a trip to the liquor store on my way out of town.

I waved at Lincoln as I backed up, a feeling of guilt blooming from my chest and filling me up completely.

Lincoln represented a different option, a different route that I could have taken ... but, at this point, there was no reason to drag him down with my ship of horrors.

Chapter 15

The drive back to *The Rest EZ* was sluggish and gray. My eyes were clouded with sleep, my mouth watering from withdrawal. My legs were achy, temples throbbing ... pulsating strikes that vibrated the syllables of her name: *Val-er-ie. Val-er-ie.*

No matter how hard I try, I can't shake her.

It was nearly evening, so I'd have to pay for another day at the motel. I still had to pack up my few meager belongings and figure out where to go next.

Inside the motel room, I stripped off my clothes and stepped into the cramped shower stall. It was barely big enough to bend over to shave in, but luckily, I'd left my razor at home. I'd gotten lazy when it came to showers—*what is the point, after all? I'm not sleeping with anyone. No one touches my legs, or the rest of my body for that matter.*

There was no one to gross out with my poor hygiene practices.

Well, there was Lincoln ... but I'd probably never see him again.

I washed with the dry, generic motel soap, letting the hot water wash over my head in sudsy waves. There were tangles of slimy blonde hair pooling around the drain ... *Valerie's? They must be.* I tried to nudge them down the drain with my big toe, but as soon as one disappeared, I'd find another one, tickling the pads of my feet.

Oh, Valerie. Why won't you get out of my head? And why do I care so much?

I closed my eyes, rubbing my hands over my breasts and stomach, trying to imagine what it must feel like to be her in the shower.

But my hands quickly found the grooves of scar tissue; *nope, I'll never know what it feels like to have smooth skin again,* I thought, bitterly.

I tried to focus on scrubbing, the acrid bar of soap burning my eyes and skin as I rubbed too hard.

Like the hair in the drain, my mind kept circling back to Valerie.

The tiny bathroom was filling up with steam, and I found that I was too hot ... and thirsty, even though I'd drunk a liter of soda with Lincoln at the garage.

I slipped as I climbed out of the shower, skinning my knee on the door. I opened my mouth to scream, but nothing came out, then I eased myself down onto the floor, clutching my red, raw wound.

That's when I saw the blood. It was light, almost pink, swirling around the drain ... dripping down the side of the tub. It took a moment for my brain to catch up ... *No way I'd bled that much; it was just a small abrasion ...*

I looked up—the blood was coming from overhead ... *drip drip drip.* The black T-shirt Valerie had left behind, the one that was damp, hanging over the towel bar the first day ... it had gotten wet again from my shower.

Creepy-crawlies tickled my scalp as I stepped onto the toilet lid and, cringing, lifted the shirt from the bar. I got back down and knelt beside the shower, holding the heavy wet shirt over the drain. I squeezed the thick cotton fabric, staring in horror as blood trickled down my wrists and spilled between my fingers ...

Chapter 16

I'd calculated the distance between Paducah and Gatlinburg—it was less than four hundred miles away. Technically, I could make it to Tennessee faster than I could get back home.

Home. What a stupid word.

Oshkosh is not my home.

Besides my sister, I had no family there. My old "family", the one I married into, wanted nothing to do with me. Now they were accusing me of not only stealing my husband's ashes, but a priceless heirloom *and* a deadly weapon to boot.

Fuck Oshkosh.

It was one thing for the Browns to hate me—but the entire town?

I don't want to go back to that tomb of an apartment. I thought about the shit-brown walls and the hypnotic hum of my refrigerator. The swishing sound of those fan blades above my bed ... the loneliness that threatened to eat me alive, whether I was home or elsewhere ...

I was wasting away in that dump. I can't stay here, but I can't go there either.

Something stirred in the pit of my stomach, and it wasn't the scream this time. What was it ... *excitement, fear, determination?*

Valerie Hutchens was perfect. But her life certainly wasn't. She'd been hurt before she left town ... by the same person who'd hurt her aunt? Did he kidnap her and take her to Tennessee?

I took my cell phone out and unblocked my sister's number. Then I punched in the letters to spell the words, then entered in the number I'd known for half my life.

Me: I love you, Hannah. But I can't come back. There's nothing left for me there.

Taking a deep breath, I clicked send, then re-blocked her. *Goodbye, Hannah.*

My clothes were spread out around the room, lumpy landmines of sweat-stained tops and two-day-old underwear. I needed some new ones, or at the very least, a place to wash them clean.

"This time I won't forget to pack you," I said, scooping up the box of ashes. I buried the box deep in my bag, then turned around to look at the bed. Chris was under the covers, the sheets tucked all the way up to his chin. His mouth didn't move, but his eyes followed me around the room as I finished packing.

I blinked once, twice, willing him to go away. I was tired and foggy from the lack of sleep and withdrawals, so much so that it was hard to tell if I were asleep or dreaming ...

"I have to go," I told him, zipping my bag shut tight. Chris's pupils were large black pools, murky reservoirs of pain. He blinked but didn't respond.

I was standing at the door, staring at his ghost, when my phone started ringing. After texting Hannah, I half-expected it to be her. But then I remembered: I'd blocked her.

I stared at the number on my screen. It was one I didn't recognize—an 865-area code.

"Hello?" I answered, my own voice unfamiliar and strange.

My eyes were still on Chris, unmoving beneath the covers. He seemed to be listening.

"Camilla Brown?"

"Speaking ..." I said, holding my breath.

"Listen, I only have a second ... it's me," the woman said. "It's Valerie."

I would have recognized her voice anywhere.

"Are you okay?"

Valerie made a noise—a cross between a cry and a giggle.

"No, I'm not ... he killed my aunt and now he's going to kill me, too."

"Who? Tell me where you are and I'll call the police," I said, gripping the phone so tightly my knuckles went white.

"You can't. For some reason, they think I'm involved. Just come. I don't know where I am exactly, but I'm in

Gatlinburg. He's working at a bar across from the Black Bear Inn, but he only leaves me for short periods of time ... please come. I'll call you again if I can."

"Valerie! Describe to me where you are ... I need to know more—"

But just like that, she was gone.

Chapter 17

I was stuffing my bag in the backseat of the truck when the door to room 12 swung open. After the weird Chris hallucination, I half-expected it to be him ... chasing me like a phantom, trying to stop the inevitable.

But it was a lanky brunette with multi-colored eye shadow. She slunk out the door of room 12 and closed it behind her. She waltzed over to me, arms swinging carelessly at her sides. She was young, barely eighteen. The crooks of her arms were marked by her curse—deep track marks that looked as though they'd healed a few times, then been reopened.

"Bum a smoke?" she asked, smiling tightly back at me.

"Sure." I tossed her the pack. "I'm kind of in a hurry here. Sorry." I watched her light the cigarette, noting how skinny and pale she was.

"You been staying here long?" I asked, shoving the bag in the cramped backseat.

"Couple weeks, I guess." She was pretty, in a haunted, Courtney Love sort of way.

She took a long drag, then blew a cloud of smoke in my face. She studied my scars, starting at the ones on my nose and following the hideous trail to my chin. "Why? Who wants to know?"

"Just me, I guess. I'm looking for a friend of mine. She was staying in room 14 several days ago. She left with a man ... did you see her? I wondered if she mentioned where she might have been going next? Or if you noticed what she was driving ...?"

Two long curls of smoke seeped from each of her nostrils, like a mad bull. She glanced over at the closed door to my room. I thought about Chris's ghost on the other side, then shuddered.

The girl's eyes lingered on the door for several seconds, thoughtful. *She knows something,* I realized with a start.

"What's her name? I bet I do know who you're talking 'bout."

"Valerie," I said, flatly. I checked my phone for more messages from Valerie. There were none. That terrified tremor in her voice raced through my mind. *I need to get going.*

"Blonde hair, real pretty?"

"Yep. That's her."

"Yeah. I borrowed some lipstick from her, actually. She seemed nice. Great clothes."

"Did you see a guy hanging around outside her room? She said she thought someone was following her. Peeking in the windows, too."

The young girl's eyes never changed. If she was surprised

by this, she didn't show it. "It was probably Bruce, the manager. He's a real perv. He'll fuck anyone, and he's always slinking around here at night. But yeah, there was a guy ... I saw him once or twice."

"Is this him?" I flipped my phone towards her and showed her the picture of the guy at the concert, holding my breath as she looked.

She nodded. "Yep. Sure is."

Fear knocked around in my chest. *What had caused the blood on Valerie's T-shirt? Did he beat her up before taking her ...?*

"Do you know what kind of car she was driving? And him—what was he driving?"

"Uhhh ... I never saw any other vehicles besides hers. She's got a cute two-door Miata. I guess they left together when they checked out, but I'm not real sure. Don't you know what she drives? You said she was your friend ..."

"I haven't seen her in a while," I said. "And I think that car is new," I added the lie. "Did you hear anything over there ... screaming or fighting?"

She shook her head and stamped the cig out with her Reebok shoe. For someone with a drug problem, she had some really nice shoes, I noticed.

The drive to Gatlinburg, Tennessee was better than the initial drive to Paducah. I was so tired I could barely see straight, having gone nearly forty-eight hours on less than two hours of sleep.

But the rise and fall of the rocky terrain and the beautiful mountain scenery, made it all worth it. I switched lanes to get around a sluggish VW beetle. I was going as fast as I possibly could, but somehow, it didn't feel fast enough ...

I approached a knot of cars idling in stand-still traffic. We inched forward, entering what looked like a cloud of smoke that clung to the ridges of the Smoky Mountains.

I could barely see the gray van in front of me, inching along and quickly slamming on my brakes as the taillights appeared by surprise like two round cat eyes. My pulse was quickening, memories of the bone-crunching smash of the backend of that semi's trailer with the Buick invading my thoughts ...

I wiped sleep from my eyes, fighting to keep them open as I chugged a Polar Pop mixed with soda and vodka. Drinking was a bad idea, but it was having a calming effect, which I so badly needed right now.

The broad white sign for Gatlinburg emerged from overhead and I scrunched up my neck, looking up to make sure it was real and not a mirage. Even though it was October, there were neon Christmas lights and what looked like Christmas trees on either side of the sign. I was seeing double; the tree lights were a smudgy smear in the distance.

Traffic was still thick, everyone trying to make it into the narrow strip of shops and restaurants that lined the main touristy center of town. A ski lift carrying couples, feet dangling wildly, clanked loudly overhead. I was mesmerized by all the walking bodies, on both sides of the strip and

Like, Follow, Kill

crossing the road ... *How will I ever find Valerie in this mess?*

I followed the signs for free parking and room vacancies, finally relieved to make a sharp right into a skinny alleyway off the strip.

Traffic was too thick to drive, so I left the truck near a Days Inn parking lot and followed the throngs of people walking. They looked cheery, with their shopping bags and strollers full of snotty children. I passed six candy shops along the way, one that was making big creamy strings of taffy in the front window. My stomach groaned. I'd probably lost five pounds since leaving Oshkosh. I needed some food in my stomach, and I needed a bed to sleep in. But first, I needed to find the Black Bear Inn and this bar across the street from it.

But hunger is a nasty thing—my stomach grumbled loudly as I walked. The last thing I'd eaten was that sloppy sandwich from the gas station Lincoln bought me.

Lincoln.

Guilt festered inside me—he had messaged and called today. He'd even offered to come along and help me look for my friend. He obviously knew I'd been lying when I said I was going back home. *Is my desperation that obvious to everyone?*

But I'd ignored all his messages and calls ...

In another version of my life story, maybe I would have let him come. Maybe I'd have chosen the path where I let him help me, where he became my boyfriend and loved me despite all my dark and cloudy bullshit ... but I liked him a little *too* much. His hands were soft, and his smile was kind ... but he looked and acted nothing like Chris ... *he's not Chris.*

And it was too soon ... and in this version, the *real* version of my life, I didn't need a Lincoln, or anyone else, to come along and save the day. I had to find Valerie all on my own.

I'm going to be the hero of this fucking story ... god knows I've been the villain long enough.

I could see the tall gray hotel I'd snapped a picture of online. The Black Bear Inn hovered over the shops in the distance. I still needed to go back and get the truck, but at least while I was here, I could see if there were rooms available.

The bar across the street was dark. *It's barely midnight, and they're already closed?!*

The man at the counter of the Black Bear Inn was cheery and bright, and I could have kissed him when he said there was one room left for the night. I told him I'd take it, before inquiring about price. *Money doesn't matter anyway; I'll probably be in jail soon,* I thought, as I regretfully shelled out the hundred-dollar deposit and took my key to the room.

"Why is the bar across the street shut down so early?" I asked the man.

He smiled, his eyes avoiding my face. "Can't serve alcohol after midnight here. Sorry, it's the law. It'll be open tomorrow, though."

"That's a stupid law," I snapped. As much as I wanted to find Valerie's stalker, I'd also been looking forward to another drink while I was there, scoping him out.

"There's a mini bar in your room," the receptionist said, frowning.

"Thank god," I muttered.

Room 447 was nicer than my dinky room at *The Rest EZ*. The bed was king-sized, the walls white and clean, and there were no ghosts waiting in the shadows for me.

The windows were too high up for anyone to see in and the curtains were tightly drawn. For the first time in days, I felt alone. But at the same time, I was also scared ... scared that someone was hurting Valerie while I sat here, helpless, and drunk, in a cushy hotel room.

I looked over at my bag, wishing I'd remembered to bring the box with Chris inside with me. He was still planted on the passenger's seat of the truck.

I picked up a menu for room service, finally settling on an order of chicken wings and curly fries. I also chose a bottle of overpriced Grey Goose from the mini bar.

While I waited, I searched for updates in the news, on Janet's murder or my pending charges, but there was nothing.

I sent another message to Valerie:

It's Camilla again. I'm in Gatlinburg. I hope you are okay. I'm staying at the Black Bear Inn, but the bar is closed. Let me know where you are if you can. I tried

that number you called me from ... no one is answering.

By the time I'd finished my food and peeled off my sweaty clothes, I was drifting off to sleep ... imagining myself floating on a puffy white cloud that overlooked the mountains, Valerie drifting by my side ...

The admission price for the House of Illusions was 29.99. I paid it gladly, wandering through the too-tight corridors, searching aimlessly for Valerie. The pictures on the walls were moving, their faces morphing into something else ... and at the end of the hallway, there was a huge white wall and a button. *"Lean here and press the button to capture your shadow,"* read the sign. I tried it, but my shadow evaporated when I moved. I pressed the button again and again, until finally, a slinky black shadow appeared. I recognized the broad shoulders and the narrow waist ... the sinewy forearms ... but the head and neck were separated from the torso, and when I touched the sheen white wall, there was blood on my fingertips. Blood in my mouth ... I can taste his blood, like a copper penny in my mouth ...

I wrestled with the hotel bedding, wrapped like a mummy in the too-thick sheets ... I rolled and fought off the material, finally collapsing onto the floor beside the bed and jerking awake. I was sweating, feverish ... remnants of the dream trickling away so fast, I couldn't catch them before they were gone.

I stripped off my underwear and bra, then locked myself in the bathroom and showered. I tried to rub the smell and feel of the blood in the dream off my subconscious ...

Finally, when I emerged from the bathroom, shivering in a fuzzy, gray towel, I saw that it was barely 7am. I was still sleepy, but at least my head felt clear. Chris's ghost hadn't shown up yet, and for once, I was thankful for that. I didn't need his accusatory eyes fixated on me right now ...

After drying my hair with the towel, I got dressed in the same clothes from last night.

I locked my room up tight, then went down to the lobby. A new attendant was working behind the counter. He greeted me and suggested I check out some of their brochures. I thanked him and stepped outside, my still-damp hair making me shiver in the hazy morning light.

I was surprised to see hundreds of people already out on the strip. A large knot of couples and families were lining up outside the pancake restaurants for breakfast, but the bar hadn't opened yet. Eventually, I settled on a small, woodsy-themed restaurant that was offering steaming cups of coffee to its waiting guests. I accepted the coffee and took a seat on a bench outside, while holding my buzzer for my "table for one".

I was tempted to smoke, but there were too many people ... I blew steam off the top of my coffee instead, watching teenagers, families, and couples pass me by on the street. I was lost in thought when I felt something vibrating in my hand. I stood up, expecting the buzzer to be going off, but instead, realized it was my cell phone.

I must have accidentally flipped it to vibrate while carrying it in my pocket. Probably Lincoln again …

Glancing down at the phone, I was surprised to see a social media update. *A new message on Instagram from Valerie!*

I stepped under the awning of the restaurant, squeezing between two families waiting to be seated. I cupped my hands around the screen protectively, squinting to read her message in the bright morning sunlight.

He's there now, across the street.

I quickly wrote back:

Who?

But I knew the answer already … her stalker.

Where are you? I want to help. You should tell the cops.

Another quick response:

No. Don't do that.

My rumbling stomach all but forgotten, I wandered down the sidewalk, waiting for her to say more but knowing she wouldn't.

Where is he? At the bar already? It's not open yet. Where are YOU?

One minute passed, then two. I paced up and down the sidewalk, oblivious to the crowds of people trying to swerve around me.

Finally, my phone buzzed again.

I don't know where I am.

I typed back quickly:

Can you describe it?

I plopped down on an open bench, realizing that I'd

wandered two blocks from the restaurant even though I still had one of their buzzers. I waited for fifteen minutes for a response from Valerie, then finally got up and walked back toward my hotel.

The sparkling lights of an arcade were lit up across the street, next to the bar. It was open.

Through the milky-white glass, I looked inside the arcade. There was a small pizza stand, serving pizza by the slice. The big gooey slices looked almost as big as my head. My own face reflected back at me, and it wasn't only the sight of my scars that repelled me. My eyes were hooded, blue-black moons underneath, my cheeks hollow. I looked like a walking skeleton, only scarier.

A flash of shiny black hair behind me in the street caused me to turn.

I'll be damned. What are the odds of that?

My eyes locked on the man instantly. He was across the street, strolling out of the whiskey bar. I stared at him, unmoving as people passed me by on the sidewalk. He glanced left then right, his eyes glazing over mine for a split second, then he crossed the street, coming toward me.

I stepped below a shadowy awning between the arcade and a shop that sold cheesy, air-brushed T-shirts. The Chris lookalike brushed right past me, and I held my breath as he did. He *did* look like Chris, but also not. His hair was dark like his, but he was shorter and lankier. He was younger than Chris. But I had no doubt—this was the man I'd seen in Valerie's video ... the same man that had also appeared in the background of two of her photos. The man who was holding her captive now, apparently.

I willed my feet to move, to follow him ... *This might be my only chance!*

I bobbed and weaved through the thickening crowds, not taking my eyes off the back of his head. He was walking briskly, his tanned arms swinging side to side, like he didn't have a care in the world.

Then suddenly, he stopped walking. For a moment, I worried that he might sense he was being followed. But that was ridiculous—he didn't know me at all.

He glanced at a sleek black iPhone, then started walking again. I kept up the pace. When he stopped at a cross walk, I stopped too, keeping a few people between us.

The light flashed, and then we were moving again. I was so close now, only one woman between us, and I could smell the spicy scent of his aftershave ...

The sidewalk became narrower and steeper, and suddenly, I realized where he must be headed ... a large parking garage. Under my breath, I cursed myself for leaving my truck by the Days Inn last night. *If he gets in a car, I won't be able to follow him!*

As suspected, the Chris lookalike turned into the wide mouth of the parking garage. There was a young couple between him and I, and as they turned into the same garage, I breathed an internal sigh of relief, following behind.

Inside the garage, I held back as I watched him approach a concrete stairwell that led to the next floor up. The couple, unfortunately, were parked on level one. They split off, and then it was just me ... following the man up the twisty staircase. I took my keys out of my pocket, and taking my time, I filed up the heavy set of steps, praying he didn't turn back and think anything of the strange, scarred woman coming up behind him.

On the second level of the garage, I was so close I could touch him, and I was surprised he didn't turn to look. But then he stopped so quickly that I nearly collided into his backside.

"Oh! Excuse me," I said. I kept walking, barely breathing, and I forced myself to wait several seconds before glancing back at him over my shoulder.

When I did, I saw him standing beside a large black Range Rover. He was looking right at me now, a puzzled expression on his face.

Heart racing, I started looking around the too-quiet lot, pretending that I couldn't find my car. Then I heard the slam of a car door and an engine turning. He's leaving!

When his Range Rover pulled out, I started walking back in his direction. I repeated the license plate out loud over and over, scrambling to get my phone out so I could write it down in time.

Chapter 18

B ack in my hotel room, I scurried under thick, flannel blankets, shaking. I'd missed my chance to find her ... I was unprepared, not expecting to run into the stalker so soon.

In the pitch-black room, I held up my phone, reading off the numbers again. I'd written them down in the notes section on my phone. My first inkling had been to message Valerie again, tell her I had the creep's license-plate number. But it had seemed too strange, running into the guy as soon as I got to the bar, almost like he knew I was looking for him ... and Valerie still hadn't responded to my last message.

I was afraid to tell her the truth—that I had failed.

I typed out a message to Lincoln. I'd been thinking about it the whole walk back to my hotel room, and if anyone could help with this, it was him.

Me: You told me that you have friends in the police force? Do you think you could do me a huge favor and have them to look up a license plate for me? This is really important, or I wouldn't ask.

Hoping for a fast response, I was disappointed when hours passed, and I still hadn't heard anything. I'd turned the TV on in my hotel room. Numbly, I flipped through channels, feeling a sad aching for that shitty motel room in Kentucky, Valerie's smell on the blankets and her corny Netflix shows on the screen.

The stations here were mostly local, a series of one advertisement after another that offered activities for guests in Gatlinburg. My head was buzzing with adrenaline—*Who is this creep? Why has he taken Valerie?*

I closed my eyes, picturing the headline in the *Oshkosh Gazette*: *Local loser tracks down killer and saves the day.*

I nearly laughed out loud at my own foolish imagination.

I picked at a stray string on the comforter, winding it around and around my finger, thinking about how good it would feel to have my pain medication. At least I had a drink to keep me company ...

My cell phone rang beside me and I jerked upright to a sitting position. I had expected Lincoln to text back, not call, but I was relieved to hear from him.

I tucked my knees up to my chest, then answered his call.

"Hey. Thanks for calling me back," I said, quietly.

"You okay? Whose license plate am I looking up?" Lincoln sounded antsy, like me, but there was something soothing about hearing his voice again.

"The creep that's been following my friend. I was thinking maybe you knew someone ..."

"I do. Not sure if he'll do it or not but give me the

number and I'll give it a try. It's Saturday, so not sure how quick I can get through to him though."

Although that was disappointing to hear, I was still thrilled to hear that he was willing to give it a try. I read the numbers and letters off slowly, then repeated them just to make sure.

"Will you call me back when you find out something?"

"Will do. Camilla?"

"Yes?" I asked, releasing the too-tight string on my finger.

"You should let me come to you. I can't shake the feeling that you're in some kind of trouble. I know this sounds weird, but I feel like we're kindred spirits or something ... I know how hard it is to overcome trauma, that's all I'm saying ... it changes you, it really does."

I swallowed down a lump in my throat, sticky and hard like peanut butter, and willed myself not to cry. "I know. It's just ... there are some things you have to do on your own, you know?"

Lincoln was quiet for a minute. "Yeah, I know."

I hung up the phone, a strange wave of sadness sparking inside me. I was attracted to Lincoln, but he wasn't Chris. *No one will ever be Chris,* I realized.

I was back out on the main strip, watching for the stalker, hoping he'd return to the bar. It was nearly dark now ... the chances of him showing up this late, were slim to none. I couldn't help feeling like he'd slipped through my fingers ... *I let him get away, and in doing so, Valerie got away too ...*

My phone rang in my pocket, giving me a jolt.

"Find out anything?" I asked, relieved to see Lincoln's number.

"Yeah ... but I'm not sure if it's what you're looking for."

I plopped down on a bench outside the whiskey bar, waiting for Lincoln to tell me more.

"It's a Tennessee license-plate number and it belongs to a guy named Chris Jared. He has a few minor traffic offenses and one thing that stands out on his record."

"What is it?" I asked, my mind racing.

"Well, he has a restraining order against him."

I knew it! The guy is a total creep!

"The woman who took out the restraining order ... is her name Valerie?" I asked.

"Nope. Her name is Kelly Jared and it's his ex-wife. They both took out restraining orders on each other during the divorce. And I dug around a bit ... he used to work for Rook Pharmaceuticals. Didn't you say your friend was a pharmacy tech there?"

"A pharmaceutical rep," I corrected him. "So, they know each other, then ... this isn't some stranger following her around. It's someone she has a connection to ... someone she is afraid of for a reason." My thoughts drifted back to the bloody T-shirt in the bathroom at *The Rest EZ*. I'd tossed it in the dumpster in the back of the building, unsure what else to do with it.

"Anything else on his record?" I pressed.

I can't believe his name is Chris. They share the same

name and kind of look alike ... how creepy. A bizarre coincidence, that's all.

"That's all I know. I do have an address though."

"An address?! Give it to me, please."

"Well, you should encourage her to call the police. Don't approach this guy, or try to be the hero, Camilla. He could be dangerous ..."

I shook my head back and forth, waiting for the address.

"Camilla?" Lincoln said again.

"I'm here. Just thinking. I won't go to the guy's house, I promise. I'm not that crazy."

Lincoln sighed on the other end. I could tell he didn't want to give me the address, but deep down, I knew he would.

"He lives in a cabin, I looked it up on Google Maps. The address is 636 Woodlawn Drive. It's right outside of Gatlinburg."

I memorized the address in my head, trying to stay calm. "Thank you, Lincoln. I can't tell you how much help you've been."

That familiar sense of guilt returned as I told him goodbye. I could tell that he didn't want to let me off the phone but felt like he had to.

Not for the first time in my life, I'd told a lie to someone I cared about.

The only way I could stop this Chris Jared guy was if I confronted him somehow ...

I did a quick search online for him, pulling up multiple

results. There were several men with the same name, but only one Chris Jared from Tennessee was on Facebook. As soon as I pulled up his profile pic, I recognized his dark hair and eyes, that stony gaze I'd seen on the street earlier ...

Chapter 19

For the next two hours, I tried to find out everything I could online about Chris Jared. I couldn't find a direct link between him and Valerie, although I already knew that there was one. They had worked together at Rook Pharmaceuticals at some point, according to Lincoln, which meant he definitely wasn't a stranger.

Was he an ex-lover or a friend of Valerie's? Perhaps a disgruntled former employee? Someone who is angry at her for quitting?

Lincoln was right about one thing—Chris Jared was divorced. But there was no mention of children. Both wife and husband had filed restraining orders, but there were no public details.

He lived in a cabin. A small subdivision in the Tennessee mountains called Rocky Falls. From what I could tell, his closest neighbor was miles away. It was less than an hour away from me now ...

I sat in my truck, unmoving, unsure what to do. The best thing to do would be to wait until Chris-the-stalker went to the bar, then drive up to the cabin. But he didn't seem to be coming back, and what if Valerie was running out of time ...?

And that's when my phone chimed: *Valerie messaging me back—finally!*

I gasped as I saw the photo she'd sent me. It was a selfie, her cheeks and eyes swollen and bruised.

He's going to kill me. Those five words sent chills down my spine.

If Valerie has access to a phone—even if it's only for brief periods of time—why is she wasting her time messaging me instead of calling the cops? Sure, they might think she's involved in Janet's death ... but fighting to prove her innocence is better than dying, isn't it?!

Something about this wasn't adding up.

I knew what I needed to do—call the police.

But I couldn't bring myself to do that either. *Valerie had told me not to; she must have a good reason for that. And what if the cops show up and they realize there's a warrant for me? What if I'm taken into custody before I can help Valerie? What if there is no one left to save her?*

I parked the truck illegally at the curb and jumped out, ignoring the chorus of horns behind me. I took off running, dodging people left and right on the sidewalk. They glared at my ugly face, my panicked motions ... *but I no longer care what other people think.*

"Excuse me ... please! Let me through!"

I'd seen a knife outlet next to one of the pancake

Carissa Ann Lynch

restaurants. The window had been full of sharp-looking pocket knives and swords.

If I'm going after Chris Jared, then I need to be prepared. Every hero needs a weapon ...

210

Chapter 20

Gravel crunched like old bones beneath my feet. My hands were tucked deep inside my pockets; in my right hand, I held the knife. It had a rubber handle with grooves for my fingers. It felt good in my hand, as though it had always belonged there.

I'd parked the truck a quarter mile from Chris Jared's cabin and I approached his house on foot.

I'd expected something gloomy. Rustic. But the small log cabin that Chris Jared called home looked rather new; it was small and homey, orange and yellow flowers planted in neat little rows along a stone pathway that led up to the entranceway.

It didn't look like the place where a stalker/kidnapper/possible killer might live. The closest thing to horror was a plastic skeleton dangling from the rafters on his front porch. The Halloween prop swung in the breeze, ominously.

I'd followed the directions perfectly, hadn't I?

Was it possible Chris Jared was here, holding Valerie captive? Or might he have taken her somewhere else?

I peered out from between two trees, eyes scanning every visible surface of the cabin and surrounding area. The Range Rover was parked on the side. No cute red Miatas, like the manager at *The Rest EZ* and the young girl staying there had told me.

The porch light was on, but inside the cabin was dark. *Does he have Valerie in there with him? And most importantly, is she still alive?*

But he could be watching me from the window right now, waiting for me to strike …

I forced myself to move. Emerging from the trees, I snuck stealthily around the right side of the cabin. My limbs relaxed except for the hand on the knife deep inside my pocket.

Slowly, I circled around the side, praying my footsteps were quiet enough not to disturb him or any nearby animals.

The backside of the cabin was less neat. There were no decorations or flower beds. No outdoor lighting to speak of. Gently I gripped the doorknob and twisted, a tiny shock of pleasure running through me as it turned easily in my hand.

This is easy … maybe too easy. Am I walking into a trap?

I released the knob, changing my mind, and raised my hand to knock instead. I'd barely brushed my knuckles over the surface, when the door swung open. I leapt back in surprise.

Chris Jared was wearing flannel sleepy pants. No shirt.

It took me several seconds to find my voice.

"Can I help you?" he asked, rubbing his eyes with the back of his hand. Even though it was dark outside and inside, I was able to get a good look at him in the cold moonlight. If he recognized me from earlier, he didn't let on.

He looks nothing at all like Chris, I realized. *Maybe the resemblance was all in my head.*

"I know it's late, and I'm so sorry to bother you ... but you see, my truck broke down up the road and my cell phone's dead. I was hoping I could come inside and use your phone? I'm not a psycho, I promise," I said, praying he couldn't smell the vodka on my breath.

"Yeah, of course. Come in." Once again, I thought: *Too easy.*

Chris opened the door and wandered inside the cabin, carelessly exposing his shirtless backside to me. I'd barely closed the door behind me before I'd taken out the knife.

There was no point in beating around the bush—I had to act and act fast.

The shiny new blade gleamed in the dark living room, making me feel powerful.

"Who are you, really?" I pointed the knife toward his back, holding it far enough away so I wouldn't accidentally cut myself.

Chris turned around slowly, holding up his hands in a defensive posture. "Chris Jared. Who the fuck are you?"

"Where are you keeping Valerie Hutchens? And why did you kill her aunt?"

Chris's eyes sparkled like two shiny pennies in the dark.

"I have no idea what you're talking about," he said, pronouncing each word slowly. But there was something about his eyes—they were smiling ...

"Oh, but you do. You followed her to a concert in Ohio, and then another trip to the beach ... and you followed her to Paducah and now you're keeping her against her will in Tennessee ..."

"I live here. This is my home. And I was sleeping ... I don't have anyone here. I need you to turn around and leave right now. If you know what's good for you, you'll go ..."

I moved in closer with the knife, my hand shaking wildly. "I'm not going anywhere, Chris."

He's never going to tell the truth, I realized. *I guess I'll have to force it out of him.*

"If you don't tell me where she is, I'm going to kill you. Do you understand?" I took three steps forward with the knife. He scooted back, bumping his backside against a tall, oak hutch.

"You must be a big fan of Valerie's," he said. His lips twitched.

"Not a fan. *A friend.* And I need you to tell me where she is right now."

Suddenly, his demeanor changed completely. The corners of his lips curled into a smile that matched his eyes. He took a step closer, ignoring the knife that wobbled in my right hand.

"Do you see that?" he asked, pointing at something on the wall behind him.

I glanced over my shoulder. "See what?"

"That," he said.

He was pointing at something round and dark on the wall. It looked like an everyday clock.

"The cameras," came a whisper behind me.

The voice was small but shrill, almost like a ding.

Or like a bell.

I'd know that voice anywhere; I'd heard it in my dreams so many times ... heard it only yesterday ...

Slowly, I turned around and came face-to-face with Valerie Hutchens. Her face was flawless, bruise-free, in the shadowy living room.

She grinned. And like Ms. Sauer that first day of middle school, I couldn't help myself—I smiled back.

Then Valerie slammed something big and heavy down over my head. The room grew smaller and smaller, melting into complete darkness.

Chapter 21

I opened my eyes and swallowed. The roof was spinning as I blinked back tears from the pain—my skull felt like it was being ripped from the inside out, like an angry demon clawing its way into the world.

And then it all came rushing back to me ... *I was drinking. The accident ... oh my gosh, I crashed the Buick! How could I be so stupid? Chris ...*

I glanced over at the passenger's seat, but Chris was no longer in it. There was something else, a lumpy gray mannequin, a mannequin with no head ... I recognized the shirt and pants, the jagged hole of space above his neck ... *Oh my god.*

Gasping for air, I tried to move, my arms weren't responding to my brain's commands.

I can taste blood in my mouth. Chris's blood.

I remember now: I bit him. But why the hell would I do that?

And then I remembered more: the fighting.

We were fighting about his cell phone. About that stupid

216

girl who had been messaging him again ... about the photo I'd found on his phone a couple weeks ago.

That photo will haunt me for the rest of my life ... but not as much as this moment.

From the driver's seat, I'd seen him smiling down at his phone. So many girls ... so many indiscretions ... and he didn't even have the decency to hide it anymore.

For a brief moment, I caught a glimpse of the message he was reading.

"So, which is it this week, huh? Virgins or whores?"

Chris's mouth gaped open, and then he did something I didn't expect: he tossed his head back and laughed. "What the hell are you talking about now, Camilla? Please enlighten me, since you know so much about me these days."

"The porn sites. The casual online hookups ... I know. And I know you know that I know ...

"One minute you're clicking on cherry-popper videos, the next it's the twenty-guy gang-bang bitch. So, I'm asking you right fucking now ... which is it you prefer: virgins or whores? Cause we both know you don't want me."

Chris covered his face, rubbing his hands up and down. I couldn't see or hear his laughter ... but I *felt* it.

"Every guy looks at porn, Camilla. And you know that; we had this conversation when we first started dating. And I like women, okay? You knew this when we got married. That was your dumb idea, remember? Being faithful isn't my thing, although I've been damned near close to that for you, so you should be happy ..."

"Yeah, but when we first got together, you weren't sneaking to the bathroom, looking at porn sites daily. You weren't messaging girls on dating sites. It's disturbing, really. But that's only a small part of it."

Chris uncovered his face, holding his hands out in a begging gesture. "Please explain it to me—a small part of what?"

"Nothing." I shrugged. *Arguing with him is pointless. I've known that for a while now.*

The lines in the road were growing blurry. The right tire of the Buick hit the road strips on the side. I waited for the growling of the strips to subside, before I answered: "It's just my whole life, I've been trying to understand ... try too hard, be too good ... and people say, 'You need to relax, be freer.' But cut loose and suddenly, girls become whores and sluts. You freak out if I even look at another guy, but you're free to do what you want ... I can't walk this tightrope anymore. The game is fucking rigged." I said the words so quietly, Chris asked me to repeat myself.

"Look, I saw the picture on your phone. I know about the girl you've been seeing."

"Don't start this shit again, Camilla. You know what happened last time." I remembered the sting of the blow, his hands tightening around my neck ... the silent scream that would never come ...

He was smiling back down at his phone, texting away.

Sharply, I jerked the wheel of the Buick to the left. *Now that will get his attention.*

"Hey! Don't do that!" Chris shouted. His phone fell with a thump between the seats. I smiled as I watched him scramble, desperately trying to find where it had fallen.

I can remember a time when those hands were desperately searching for me … not someone else, not squeezing my neck … not hurting me, like this.

"Don't do what?" I said, jerking the wheel to the right. I pressed my foot down hard on the gas, picking up speed.

"You're so fucking pathetic, Camilla. My mom was right about you."

"Fuck you!" I shouted.

I gripped the wheel so hard my knuckles turned white. I'd had a couple drinks earlier, but my head was clear. *Clear enough to know my marriage is over for good.*

"You fucked her, didn't you?" I asked, staring blearily at the road in front of me. Tears were filling up; I widened my eyes, trying to stop them from spilling over. "I know you did. I saw the photo on your phone. I know you've been seeing her."

"I have no idea what you're talking about, Milly. Seriously! But I'm glad you brought all this up."

"Oh yeah? Why's that?" I said, flatly, swerving from side to side.

"Because I'm not in love with you anymore."

Now it was my turn to laugh.

219

"Look, you need to slow down, okay? You're scaring me right now. Have you been drinking?"

"How good of you to notice," I said, chuckling.

Chris reached for the wheel, and like a wild animal, I jerked my head over and bit down—*hard*—on his arm.

"Ow! What the fuck? You bit me!"

"I was crazy for loving you. And even more crazy for putting up with your family ..." I pressed down harder on the gas, my speed jumping up to 80 miles per hour.

The tears threatening to tumble loose came gushing out and I eased my foot off the gas.

It's over between us. I've known it for a while, but now there is no longer any doubt.

I released my hands from the wheel. *I want to float through life, just like Valerie Hutchens. See where this shitty road takes me.*

"Camilla, look out!"

A truck merged into the left-hand lane. *I don't have enough space to brake!*

The Buick skidded across the pavement.

I woke up to the sounds of metal and pavement, pain coursing through my head and back. I stared up at the roof. It was no longer made of metal, but slats of wood ... *I'm not in the Buick, am I?*

I recognized the log walls of the cabin, and when I turned my head to the right, I had a sideways view of the kitchen. I was laying on the floor in Chris's living room.

Not my Chris, but the stalker Chris: Chris Jared. And he'd hit me over the head with something ... *No, wait, it wasn't him. It was Valerie.*

"Good morning, Sleeping Beauty." I turned my head to the left and came face to face with a pair of untied Reeboks. My eyes followed the shoes up to the long, tan, slender legs that connected them to the girl. Valerie was sitting on the couch, smiling, one leg crossed over the other.

"Rise and shine," she said, grinning like a Cheshire cat. Her face didn't have any bruises on it.

"What the fuck is going on?" I croaked. My voice was throaty, not my own.

"Welcome to my YouTube channel. As my number-one fan, you are the guest star of episode one. Surprise!"

"Come again?" I tried to sit, but the room was spinning. *Do I have a concussion?*

"I knew you'd come. You took a little longer than I hoped, but still ... you're a true follower, Camilla."

"Why did you hit me? I came to help ..."

"Look, I'm sorry about that. I was worried you were going to stab Chris for real. That would have ruined everything. We have so much great footage, and I can't wait to share our story." She laughed so loud; it was almost like a shout. I winced, the grating sound of her voice like nails on a chalkboard now.

"Come on, Camilla, tell the truth. Did you really come all this way to help me? You barely know me, and my guess is that you don't really like me anyway."

"That's not true ... I did. I used to ..." I tried to focus on her bright-blue eyes and shiny hair ... seeing her in person felt surreal and all too real, at the same time. She didn't look like she did in her pictures. She had aged dramatically; her face no longer that of a young, carefree girl. Now she was a determined woman, a woman with a dirty plan and an awful laugh. *Valerie Hutchens, unfiltered.*

"People don't watch the news anymore, Camilla. And they don't read books or newspapers either ... no one cares about real information; they believe what they want to see. What they're *told* to see. You saw a girl you admired, a girl who was in trouble ... and based on that alone, you wanted to come to my rescue. It's not enough to have followers anymore, you understand that, right? Sure, my followers like my photos and make their stupid comments ... but would they really *follow* me, huh? Would they come to my rescue if I needed them?"

"So, Chris wasn't really stalking you? But I saw him in the video ... and in the photos ... he was watching you through the window ..."

"He was in the photos because I put him there. We've been traveling together for ages. And the stunt in the window was just a prank. I wanted to get a reaction out of you. Out of all of you. Congratulations; you definitely passed the test."

"Test? What fucking test? Why would you pretend you had a stalker?" I asked, incredulously. I wasn't mad exactly, just confused. *Was Valerie this desperate for attention?*

222

"I had a stalker once, but nobody believed me. Nobody cared enough to help me then."

"I'm sorry, I don't understand, and my head hurts really freaking bad. I'm not thinking clearly. Do you have anything to drink?" I coughed and sat up, finally managing to prop myself up on my elbows.

"That guy finally moved on to someone else. But he's always stuck with me ... and so, I'm making a new channel about followers and what they're willing to do to reach me—what can I make people believe, Camilla? I'm starting to think they'll believe anything. After all, you believed that Chris killed my aunt."

I groaned, pulling myself up all the way. I wrapped my hands around my knees, the lightheadedness subsiding slightly as I sucked in shallow, craggy breaths. "Then who did kill her? Was it you?"

"Nobody, silly. My aunt is alive and well in Oshkosh. She's completely fine."

"No, that's not true ..."

"Yes. You never saw it on the news, did you?"

I shook my head, trying to shake off the prickly stars sprouting from behind my eyelids. I felt like I might vomit.

"The manager at *The Rest EZ* told me she was murdered. The cops were there looking for you ..."

"The manager at *The Rest EZ*, huh? Good ol' Bruce. It's amazing what people will do when they're obsessed with you. I've been staying at that dump for free for years. He's related to our old school pal, Luke. Do you remember him?"

She went on, giving me no chance to respond: "Whenever I pass through town, I stay there. I always hoped Aaron would worry about my safety there, that he might be the one looking for me ... but, oh well. He's not a true follower, not worthy of my time. Bruce played into my plan, perfectly. I told him what to say, and he did it. Pretty simple, actually." Valerie shrugged, looking all too pleased with herself.

"Your aunt is worried about you ... people are looking for you ..."

Valerie was staring at her nail beds. She bit off a hangnail and spit it on the floor beside me.

"My aunt knows I'm fine. I called her. And no one is looking for me ... Bruce lied about my aunt, the cops. He's a loyal friend. But a true follower? The verdict's still out on that one."

"Are you telling me that all of this was a lie? For what, Valerie? Why the fuck would you do this? You don't even know me."

"You're right. I don't know you at all. You're just a nobody to me. But that didn't stop you from stalking my page, liking all my posts, following me across the country ... pretty much harassing me! This is going to make such a good first episode. I'm thinking about doing a scavenger hunt each month ... kind of like *Where's Waldo?* only it'll be *Where's Valerie?* And I'm going to challenge people on what they think happened versus reality ... I enjoyed watching you sulking in your motel room. And the bloody shirt ... that was fucking classic! You were so freaked out by that."

224

"What do you mean?" I stared at her in wide-eyed horror.

"There were cameras on you in the motel the whole time. And I had others, too, capturing you around town. You've been so worried about me, Camilla ... it's really sweet, actually. But you need to curb that drinking problem ..."

"Jesus," I muttered, bile rising in the back of my throat. I swallowed it down, shaking my head from side to side in disgust. *Who is this psycho bitch? Not the girl I thought I was following, that's for sure ... I underestimated Valerie Hutchens.*

"And we caught your grand finale, too—swinging that knife around at Chris. It's going to get so many views, just you wait and see. You threatening to kill Chris, a man you didn't even know, all to protect me. I'm going to tell my viewers the whole story. This will be good for both of us, Camilla. You'll be famous! It'll definitely go viral, no doubt."

I couldn't see any cameras in the dark, but somehow, I could feel them there.

"Okay, your stupid prank goes viral ... then what?"

"People love hearing shit like this about social media stars. They'll be putty in my hands after I pull this off."

"Star? I'd hardly call you a star because of your followers. Girls like you are a dime-a-dozen, Valerie." I couldn't help it; I laughed, and then I started choking. My head felt like it was on fire.

"Oh, just wait and see. Once I have my YouTube presence going, I'll be able to get the book deal I've always wanted ... I'm writing about a girl who will do anything to achieve fame. Sounds familiar, right? All of this is such good research for the book ... and I'll totally have my followers in place before it's released. Trust me, everyone will want to read this shit when it's done."

"So, what now?" I said, exasperated. "Are you going to kill me on camera or something? Is that the final scene in this twisted shit show of yours?"

Valerie laughed, deep and raucous. "Of course not. I'm not crazy, Camilla. This is it for now ... unless you're up for a post-interview tonight?"

"I think I'll pass," I said, managing to pull myself up to my feet.

On the floor beside the sofa, I could see a wooden baseball bat. *That must be what she hit me with. Crazy bitch.*

"I'm just glad no one was hurt. You impressed me, Camilla. You exceeded all my expectations. I was surprised you followed through, especially after all you've been through ... the drinking and the accident. Hell, maybe this whole thing will help you repair your reputation!"

"Whatever you say, Valerie." *All the times I'd dreamed of impressing Valerie ... this wasn't how I expected to do it.*

Valerie threw her arms around me, pulling me in for a hug. She smelled like sulfur and rot.

She whispered into my hair, still gripping me: "I'll have Chris walk you back to your truck. Oh, and if you try to sue me ... it won't matter. I'm going to make so much money off this channel that it will be worth it in the end. And I don't think you want the cops finding out that you were about to attempt murder, do you? After all, from what I've heard, you're already in deep shit back home. Unlike you, I follow the news—the *real* news—so I know what's actually going on."

I pulled away from her, disgusted.

I gave her one last, longing look, then I followed Chris-the-non-stalker outside.

"Your head okay? Good enough to drive?" Chris-the-faker asked me. His entire voice was different now, softer.

"My knife. Did you take it?"

He nodded. "Well, we kind of had to. You were about to stab me," he said, nervously.

"When is she going to post about this on YouTube, or has she already?"

"Nah, we have to put it all together. It'll take days to edit. I really hope you'll subscribe. She's using the same name as her Instagram account: *The World Is Mine*. Hey, thanks for being such a good sport. But maybe, in the future, you shouldn't follow strangers ... okay?"

Once again, I nodded. I was in so much pain, I couldn't choke out any more words.

I hobbled down the dirt path I'd followed earlier, feeling more defeated that I ever had.

I'd been so determined to eliminate Chris Jared and save Valerie ... *now look at me.*

The truck bloomed ahead like a beacon of hope. Thankful to be back, I let Chris wrench open the driver's door for me. Gently, I climbed inside. The keys were still hanging in the ignition.

"Sorry again about your head," Chris said. He turned around and started walking back to the cabin.

I turned the truck on, but I didn't take it out of park. Instead, I reached over and opened the glove box.

My fingers felt around in the dark, until I met the cool metal barrel of the gun. *I should have brought this with me the first time.*

I stepped back out of the truck and slammed the driver's door shut.

"Chris."

He was halfway up the path now, hands in his pockets, whistling as though he didn't have a care in the world.

When he heard me say his name, he turned around, squinting wearily in the gleaming white headlights of the truck.

I raised the gun and fired one shot.

Chapter 22

Chris's body lay slumped on the ground. I nudged him with the toe of my boot, holding my breath. He didn't move, and from where I stood, I could see a halo of dark-red blood spreading out on the ground beneath him. *Sorry, Chris #2.*

Satisfied he was dead, I slunk through the shadows like a ghost, avoiding the lights of the cabin as I drew near.

Surely, Valerie heard the gunshot. Any minute now, she'll come running out … shell-shocked and afraid …

But, no—as I returned to the cabin, I could hear the thumping base of hip-hop music playing loudly inside. *She is celebrating her victory.*

Celebrating my demise.

The music only grew louder as I approached the back-door. It was still ajar from when Chris and I had left earlier … *Good, this will be easy. Too easy …*

But then two white lights came rushing toward me, gravel dust flying around wildly. I watched in horror as the vehicle stopped right behind Chris's limp body on the ground.

The lights flipped off, then I heard the slamming of a car door. I pressed my back against the side of the cabin, watching.

And then I saw his scruffy hair, those dweeby professor's shoes ... Lincoln was bent down over Chris's body. He was checking for a pulse.

Fuck.

Lincoln stood up and turned around in circles. *He obviously knows I'm here—he must have passed my truck on the way in.*

There's no other choice.

I have to tell him the truth.

I emerged from the shadows and stepped into the light. Clearing my throat, I said, "Lincoln."

"Oh my god!" He came running toward me, his face glimmering with relief. "Are you okay, Camilla?"

"I feel better now."

He stopped six feet away from me, staring down at the gun in my hand. I tried to tuck it behind my back, but it was too late for that.

"What happened?" His eyes widened in fear.

"I had no other choice." There was no time to make up a lie. Maybe if I told him the truth, he'd understand ...

"It was all a prank, Lincoln. A horrible, stupid, mean prank. A way for Valerie to make fun of me, to use my desperation to gain more followers ..."

"Huh?" Lincoln's face scrunched up in confusion.

"I couldn't let him live," I said, solemnly. "I can't let her live either."

230

Lincoln took a few steps back and started digging for something in his pocket. For a brief second, I almost expected him to pull out a gun. Instead he held up his shiny black cell phone.

"I'm calling for help, okay?"

I shook my head and raised my gun. "No. I can't let you do that. Why the fuck did you come here anyway?"

Lincoln frowned. "I had to. I was worried about you. I had a feeling you'd come here, from the moment you messaged me the license-plate number."

"You shouldn't have come," I snapped.

"Listen. It's going to be okay; I promise. We'll explain what happened to the police. We will figure this out."

Looking at his face, the soft, worried expression in his eyes ... I almost believed his intentions. *I think he likes me ... he really does.*

And maybe in another life, another alternate reality of this shit show ... maybe we could have had something. Another route, another choice ...

"I'm sorry," I told him.

Lincoln froze, the phone still gripped in his hand. "Sorry for what?"

"For everything." I raised the gun and fired a second shot.

Chapter 23

Her back was to me as I stepped inside and tiptoed through the kitchen. She was wearing low-slung jeans and a cable-knit sweater. From behind, she almost looked like the girl I once knew, and admired, from high school.

Valerie was squatting down in front of a tripod. The lace trim of her thong was sticking out the top of her jeans.

Cocking my head to the side, I watched her struggle to disconnect an expensive-looking video camera from the tripod's base. The music was pounding in my ears, the thrum of it bouncing around the inside of my skull like a loose tin can. I'd never been much of a dancer, but for the first time in my life, I felt the urge to shake my hips, let the music take control ...

"About time! I need your help with this ..."

When Valerie stood up and turned around, she was grinning.

That smile. Valerie's right—she is a star. Smiles like that make people famous every day.

I'd dreamed about that smile for so many years. Hell,

I'd even imitated it in my bathroom mirror ... so many times. And I used to think that smile was genuine, but now I could see that it was anything but—*it is practiced.*

Like a hungry lion, Valerie knew how to seduce her prey. I'd fallen for her nice-girl routine—hook, line, and sinker. *Unfortunately for her, she also fell for mine.*

We all know I'm not a nice girl. I made that clear from the start.

Valerie's smile froze in place when she realized it was me, not Chris.

"Were you sleeping with Chris?" I asked her, my voice steadier than it had been in a while.

She placed her hands on her hips. "What do you mean?"

"I mean what I said. Were. You. Sleeping. With. Chris."

Valerie gave me a look of mocked confusion.

"And we both know that I don't mean that fool outside. I mean my husband. Were you sleeping with my husband, Valerie?"

"How can you ask me that? It's absolutely ridiculous! I didn't even know your husband. Look, I heard about what happened ... the accident and all ... but I barely knew the guy ..."

"But that's not exactly true, is it? A couple weeks before the accident, I saw a picture of you on his phone. You were standing on a staircase, looking down at him. You had this look in your eyes ... so intense. And he was messaging back and forth with someone. I've known all along it was you."

233

"Whoa." Valerie held up her hands and stepped closer to me. "Listen, Camilla … you are so wrong about that."

"Don't," I said gruffly, jerking away as she tried to touch me. "Keep your hands off me. Were you, or weren't you? I need to know. This is your chance to tell me the truth."

Valerie's eyes flickered up to the ceiling.

She's thinking. What the fuck is there to think about?!

"Chris Brown … yeah. I met him once, okay? He was a carpenter, right? He came over and gave an estimate to my aunt. I was there and I helped her look it over, that's all it was."

"An estimate?" My voice was becoming shaky, unsure. "What kind of estimate?"

"He was going to rebuild her staircase. That's it. My aunt thought the price was too high. She wanted to get more quotes before she decided. So, I talked to him about it. He seemed nice enough. I didn't even realize he was your husband until I saw what happened in the paper. Camilla, I swear. You have to believe me. I never saw or spoke with him any other time than that. Hell, I'm only home once in a blue moon."

"Then why the picture?"

Valerie groaned. "He wanted to take a picture of the stairs. He said he'd draw up some schematics for my aunt to look at … you know how I am, I jumped in the picture and posed on the stairs. It was nothing, really … I barely remember that day."

"I don't believe you." But that wasn't true … I was having

doubts. *Could that have been all it was—a stupid misunderstanding?*

But then I remembered the story about the murdered aunt, the stalker ... Valerie hadn't told me the truth thus far.

"You're a liar. I can't believe anything you say."

"Look, you're right. I lied about a lot of things. But I didn't know your husband. I never had anything to do with him. I never saw or spoke to him after that day."

Her smile was widening as she reached for me again. She was so close, I could smell her fear emanating from her perfect skin.

I raised the gun, and when I did, her smile started melting. Like a Dali painting, she truly was a work of art.

A beautiful smile on a beautiful face. I tried to imagine what it would feel like to cut it, maybe take it off and try it on.

I'd like to see if it fits.

As I pointed the gun in her face, the smile disappeared completely.

Chapter 24

Twelve weeks later ...

"How does the defendant plead?"

My lawyer gave me a knowing look and we both stood, facing the judge.

Judgement day. I've been waiting a long time for this.

"I'm guilty, Your Honor."

"Very well. Is there anything you'd like to say to the court, Ms. Brown?" the judge asked.

Oh, there are many things I'd like to say to the court. But I'll be keeping those things to myself.

"Yes, Your Honor."

I turned my back to the judge and faced the row of people in the court room behind me. The room was mostly empty, my one family member not in attendance. Hannah had to work this morning. Mike had offered to come in her place, but I'd told my brother-in-law not to bother. *I knew what was going to happen next and having them here wouldn't have made a difference.*

A row of Browns stared back at me from the front row, their faces arrogant and menacing. Their hatred for me rolled off them in waves. I imagined myself, shrouded in an invisible shield, reflecting their hate back at them.

I cleared my throat and clasped my hands in front of me to keep them from trembling. I hadn't drunk a drop today, and my body was feeling it …

"I would like to say I'm sorry for what I did. I know that taking Chris's remains was disrespectful and wrong, and he wouldn't have wanted me to do that. I know that now. But I wasn't thinking. Still, there's no excuse. I feel ashamed for my actions. And I'm willing to face the consequences, whatever those might be."

Bonnie Brown rolled her eyes at me, while Chris's siblings wouldn't even look me in the eye at all. Their faces were mashed up in disgust.

I smiled my imitation-Valerie smile, slow and charming, then I turned around to face the judge.

He gave Bonnie Brown a sympathetic smile, then his eyes hardened on me.

"Grief is a funny thing," he said, his voice solemn and low. "I lost my wife a few years back and at first, I was coping without her just fine. But then, one day, it just hit me like a load of bricks. And you know what I did? I went out and bought a motorcycle. My wife would have killed me for it …

"Now, what you did, Ms. Brown … that went way beyond an impulsive purchase, but I do think that some people can understand the out-of-body experience and the unencumbered pain that comes with losing a loved one, especially in your case. Your husband's death was so sudden, so horrific ... and the ashes *have* been returned to your mother-in-law, intact, correct?"

"Yes, they have, Your Honor."

"And you still deny taking the vase, or the pot ...?" The Judge ruffled through papers from his high perch on the bench.

"Your Honor, respectfully, if my client admitted to stealing the ashes, then she would have gladly admitted to stealing the pot ... and might I remind you that Ms. Brown also accused my client of taking a gun. But that gun was later found at Bonnie Brown's residence, in her late son's truck."

My attorney was a tall, Amazonian woman, with black hair and big bushy brows. She had a voice that instilled fear in people, including me, and I decided then, that she was worth the three grand I'd paid her. Selling the truck had been hard, but I'd do it again if given a second chance.

"Very well, then. Ms. Brown, I am going to let you off easily today. I hope that as you move forward, you will consider undergoing some kind of counseling, perhaps seek out some group support ...? There are groups you can attend for bereaved spouses ... they helped me tremendously. And with that said, I'm ordering you to pay a 500-dollar fine. That is all."

A chorus of groans rang out behind me, but I didn't

look back. I refused to give them the satisfaction. *They have their damn box back, what more do they want?*

I shook hands with my lawyer and thanked her repeatedly. Then I waited for the Browns to file out, one by one, before walking out of the courtroom alone.

I couldn't help feeling like I'd gotten away with murder.

Chapter 25

One year later ...

Moving boxes were stacked in the corner of the cabin, collecting dust. I needed to unload them, but there was no reason to rush ... I had my furniture in place and most of the things I needed, and I didn't plan on having company over any time soon.

The sun was rising over the mountains, an orange, seeping glow that cast rainbow prisms all over my new home.

One good thing that came out of my trip to Tennessee: I'd fallen in love with the mountains, and the subdivision where Chris Jared had once lived.

I opened the front door and stepped outside, letting the warm Tennessee sunshine color my face. *Sometimes, for a split second, it feels damn good to be alive.* Lately, I'd been consumed by these flashes of euphoria, like everything was finally coming together. Pieces of a jigsaw falling in place.

This was my favorite time of day—the rustic scent of

240

fir trees and magnolia blossoms in my backyard, and the fact that there were no neighbors around for miles.

It was quiet here—but not the kind of quiet that gave me the creeps. It felt like silence ... the peaceful kind. Up here in the mountains, you could hear a pin drop. You could also scream and never be heard.

I took my cell phone out of my back pocket and smiled at Hannah's text:

Hannah: Good morning, Milly! How are you enjoying the new place?! I'll have to set a date to come visit soon. Guess what came in the mail today?!

Cell service out here was spotty at times, and it took several minutes for the picture she had sent to load.

My lips curled into a warm smile as I stared at an image of my sister holding a book in her hands. She was covering half of her face with it, but I could see in her eyes she was proud.

The cover was haunting and beautiful, but my favorite part was my name etched in gold at the bottom. *FOLLOW ME*, the title read. By Camilla Hilbro. I'd decided to use my maiden name, and seeing it emblazoned across the cover now, I knew it was the right decision.

I wrote back to Hannah:

Me: So glad it came! I really hope you like it. Now you know why I was hiding indoors all that time ... I was busy writing! I still can't believe I pulled it off.

I didn't have any of my own copies of *FOLLOW ME* yet, but truthfully, I didn't need them. My favorite version of the story was the real one, the original—hundreds of milky-white pages written in Valerie's neat little scrawl. There were three black-and-white notebooks full of words—the story she'd been writing for years.

No one will ever know I didn't write it. It's not like Valerie can tell them.

The truth was, I did write some of it. In Valerie's version of the story, a lonely, heartless girl does anything to gain fame. It's pathetic, really. She makes the world fall in love with her, one follower at a time.

The story wasn't finished when I found it, tucked inside her pink-and-white Jan Sport backpack. My guess is that the story would have had a happy ending—the girl gains the notoriety she always wanted. All her well-laid-out plans produce the fame she desires, and she goes on to live happily ever after ... blah. *Boring.* I expected more from her, honestly.

But in my version, the girl's greed became the sword she fell upon. *Valerie didn't get the fame she wanted, not by a long shot, so why should her book character?*

Valerie did ninety percent of the work for me, but that ending ... personally, I think my ending is what made the story.

As popular as Valerie was online, no one seemed to notice her absence in real life. Her YouTube channel never came to fruition, but she did make one final Instagram post:

A mesmerizing picture of her, eyes haunted and

dark, standing by a lagoon in the Phi Phi Islands, in Thailand. Valerie was right: perception is everything! And it's amazing what you can pull off using apps like Photoshop.

It's time to disconnect for a while and focus on my writing. I won't leave until I finish my epic novel, even if it takes forever. Hope you guys understand!

#metime #byebye #sorrynotsorry

xoxoxoxo

Valerie

The photo received a few likes (including one from yours truly) and one comment from Valerie's Aunt Janet:

I will miss you, Sweetheart. But I'm so proud of you for focusing on your art and I can't wait to read your book someday.

Little did poor, resurrected Aunt Janet know—Valerie wouldn't be writing any books at all. Janet deserved better anyway—after all, Valerie had used her phantom death as a ploy for attention ...

Although I'll miss following Valerie online, she's with me all the time now. In fact, I feel like some of her magnetism floated out of her body and slipped into mine. Sometimes, when I look in the mirror, I see her face staring back at me. We do sort of look alike, I think.

Now she's my muse in the corner, always smiling, and as I get to work on book two, I know she'll stick around to help me.

Back inside the cabin, I stared down at the pile of boxes.

Just thinking about unpacking made my limbs ache. *Maybe I could unload one box today.*

First, I popped a couple pain pills. I had Valerie to thank for my pill stash as well—her little black bag of pharmaceutical samples had held me over all year and would for a few more months ...

I'd labeled each one of the boxes, to make them easier to sort through.

I dug through the pile until I found the one labeled "Chris".

"Home sweet home," I said, slicing the packing tape from the lid and taking out the beautiful, ornate water pot. It was heavier than it used to be, now that Chris was inside.

I'd returned the box to Bonnie Brown, that much wasn't a lie. But I'd carefully swapped out Chris's ashes for some other ones. You wouldn't believe how many hours you have to burn a body before it turns to ash. Especially when there's more than one to deal with ...

Since I'd re-sealed the box, Bonnie would never know the difference.

Just the thought of the Browns clustered together in their living room, worshiping their precious box, while I enjoyed my beautiful pot full of Chris, gave me butterflies of delight. Not only did she have evidence of my crimes right under her nose, but she also had the murder weapon. I didn't return the gun to its original spot beneath her bed; it would have been too risky, breaking in with those cameras out front. This time, I parked at the bottom of the hill and bypassed the cameras completely. I went to the back, to Chris's old Dodge. I used the key I still had to unlock it, and I placed the gun under the driver's seat. No one would know I put it there—except for Bonnie, of course. She claimed someone moved it—someone being me, of course—but since she's so old, no one will ever believe her.

I placed the pot on my fireplace mantle, making sure it was centered. A posy of daisies—Chris's favorite—rested beside it. *It's perfect.*

My life is perfect.

I'd used my book advance to put a down payment on the cabin, and eventually, I'd have enough money to hire a good plastic surgeon to fix my face. Then, I'd really look like Valerie ...

Inside my bedroom, I took my cell phone back out and pulled up the picture of Hannah holding *FOLLOW ME*. I sighed with pleasure.

"Would you like to see a picture of our book?"

I knelt down in front of Valerie on the floor and held the phone up in front of her face. "Isn't it pretty?"

Valerie was gagged—harder to smile that way—her hands chained to the radiator. Her big blue eyes narrowed into tiny slits as she stared at the picture.

"Look, I'm sorry about the ending. But, hey, heroes are overrated, don't you think? And just between me and you ... you're not as nice as your main character was. Not even close." Valerie was trying to say something, jerking her arms back and forth, muffled words coming through the scarf in her mouth.

"What's that, now? I can't hear you," I said, smiling.

I'd been hopeful that we could be friends ... that after a while, I'd grow on her and she'd learn to accept our life together. But truth is, it was her that wasn't growing on me ... pretty soon, I might have to let her go. Just like I did with Chris and Lincoln.

It's amazing what you can order online these days—dog cages big enough to hold humans. I'd kept her in a cage until the move; I thought she'd be happier here in the mountains, where she could move around more, with no fear of being seen.

But alas, her reaction was disappointing. Who knew that Valerie Hutchens could be such a dud?

She was still talking, struggling to voice her concerns through the thick cloth, but I was listening to something else. A sound that didn't belong here in my isolated paradise.

Gravel rumbling beneath tires brought me to the window. I peeked through the side of the blinds at a beat-up truck in my driveway. Could it be ...?

"You better stay quiet, or I'll kill you. You understand?" I pointed a finger at Valerie, my eyes wild and serious at the same time. She nodded that she understood.

I closed the door to my bedroom and tried to detangle my hair with my fingers.

I wasn't expecting any visitors, but I knew who it must be. Besides Hannah, he was the only person I'd given my new address to: *Chris.*

No, not one of the Chrises I killed, but a new one. *Chris Payne.*

Chris: Chris that I met on a dating app. He'd been pursuing me relentlessly, despite my mangled face in my photos.

I admit—it was his name that caught my attention. But not only that—*he kind of looks like my Chris. I just can't get over how much they look alike …*

I opened the door, excited to see him, but also irritated by his abrupt visit. *Don't people have manners anymore?*

My smile faded, my brain scrambling to place the familiar face …

"Hello, again. Long time no see." We had barely spoken when we were younger, but I recognized his voice. He was older now, his face more chiseled, his body more defined. *Luke. What the hell is he doing here?*

"What do you want?" I squeaked.

"You know what I want. I want to know where Valerie is. I enjoyed our little talks online."

He thrust a sharp bowie knife at my belly and I leapt back in surprise. He pushed his way inside the cabin, closing the door with a thud behind him.

"It was you on the dating app?"

Luke winked, then started looking around the cabin suspiciously.

"What do you want?" I asked, quietly.

"I knew when you posted an excerpt of your new book that it didn't belong to you. She let me read it, did you know that? All these years ... she sent me pages and pages. I read them so many times that I could recite them in my sleep."

He stepped closer with the knife. The bright-yellow sun was pouring through the drapes, reflecting off the shiny metal of his weapon.

"Oh, Luke. You weren't special. Valerie just has this way of making everyone feel like that ... it's an act. And you're wrong about the book. I wrote most of it. She gave it to me; she asked me to make sure it got published ..."

"Oh, bullshit. Valerie would never share the limelight with a loser like you. And you're wrong about me and her ... she was in love with me. Always has been."

I watched as Luke drew the blinds. My perfect cabin suddenly felt like a tomb. *My tomb.*

"You're pretty isolated out here," Luke said, smiling with all his teeth. In the bedroom, I could hear Valerie's muffled, hope-filled screams. Luke glanced over at my closed bedroom door, his eyes glowing with pleasure.

He pressed the cold, hard knife to my belly.

I guess that old saying is true—*what goes around comes around.*

As the blade tore through my skin, it felt warm ... nothing like I had imagined. Slowly, I opened my mouth.

It's time.

Like, Follow, Kill

The scream started in my belly and erupted from my throat. I'd like to think it echoed through the mountains for days ...

Finally, sweet release.

THE END

Acknowledgements

I'd like to thank my editor, Charlotte Ledger, and my agent, Katie Shea Boutillier, for championing this book. I know I already mentioned you both in the dedication, but I really can't thank you enough...

I'd like to thank the entire HarperCollins team for taking this little story on my computer and bringing it to life so that readers can enjoy it (or hate it). Specifically, thank you to Claire Fenby for tirelessly promoting my books.

Thank you to Shannon, Violet, Tristian, and Dexter for giving my life a true purpose, and meaning.

Thank you to YOU, dear reader, for taking a chance on my books. Finishing a book you've been writing is an awesome experience; seeing it as an actual book is even better. But NOTHING, and I mean NOTHING, compares to knowing that there are people like YOU out there, reading my words and enjoying (or hating) these stories that, once upon a time, only lived in my head. So, thanks for spending your time reading my words—it means more to me than I can ever express.

THE ONE
NIGHT STAND –
COMING IN 2020

Chapter 1

NOW

W hen I think about Delanie, I think about Dillan.
Three pounds, two ounces. The delivery nurse
held her out to me in the palm of her hand, like a baby
bird in its mother's nest. And right on cue, my tiny fowl
had opened her eyes and mouth, changing my life forever.

She's alive. Delanie is going to live, I'd thought. But in
those beady black eyes and chirpy pink lips ... I still saw
the son who didn't make it: *Dillan.*

There's Delanie, but no Dillan.

"Only one twin survived." That doctor's words would
haunt me for the next fifteen years, and probably longer. She
called it something ... twin-to-twin transfusion syndrome.
In layman's terms, she described it as one twin donating
blood to the other. My beautiful Delanie ... she was head-
strong and iron-willed, and it didn't surprise me that she
was the stronger of the two. Dillan's tiny heart couldn't
sustain the blood loss and he died.

So, when I woke up to find my fifteen-year-old daughter standing over me, her eyes like shiny black marbles glowing in the moonlit shadows of my room, the first thing I thought about was Dillan.

Even now, Dillan is still one of my first thoughts each morning. I wonder what he would have looked like now, as a teenager. Would he look like Delanie, with black hair and eyes, only more boyish …?

"Mom!" Delanie hissed, tugging the blankets from my chest. It's the hiss that did it—a warning sign, that Delanie's about to scream, or in the very least, get angry and throw a few things.

"W-what is it, honey? What time is it?"

My eyes fought to stay open, my contact lenses that I wasn't supposed to sleep in at night, sticking to the backs of my eyelids.

Delanie was standing up straight now, her skin so pasty and pale that it was almost translucent in the low-lit room. She had this funny look on her face.

I know that look.

Not anger, which was her go-to emotion these days … and not sadness, which was probably the runner-up … no, not either of those.

Delanie is scared. My baby girl is scared, I realized with a start. I sat up, too fast … my head swimming as I reached for her.

"What's wrong, sweetheart?"

Delanie's eyes were fixated on my bed, but she wasn't looking at me.

"There's a stranger in your bed," her words like shivery little whispers in the dark.

My scalp prickled with fear. I leapt from the bed, nearly knocking her backwards as I stared at the shape of a man. He was lying on the usually empty side of my bed.

What the hell?

He had long legs, so long they were hanging over the end of the bed. Hairy toes poked out from beneath the blankets.

He was buried beneath the sheets, except his gangly toes and a few blond pokes of hair pricking out from the top ...

My brain tried to catch up with what my eyes were seeing, but Delanie cut in: "Who the hell is he?" She took the words straight out of my mouth.

No longer was she that scared little girl I remembered from her youth ... she had transitioned back into her usual mood: angry at times, and don't-give-a-fuck mostly.

"I have no idea, Delanie."

It wasn't a lie, not exactly. I had no recollection of inviting anyone over, but it wasn't the first strange man I'd had in my bed this month ...

My mind raced, back to the last thing I remembered ... I was online again, that stupid Plenty-of-Fish site. I hadn't wanted a profile in the first place, but Pam and Jerry, my two friends from work, had set the whole thing up for me.

Did I invite one of the guys I met online to come over to the house last night? Was I drinking again … is that why I can't remember?

Suddenly, it was starting to make sense—I rarely drank alcohol, not until recently, and not since my early twenties. If I'd had a few beers last night, or even a little wine, then maybe … maybe I had blacked out completely.

But a quick scan of the room revealed no empty cans or bottles. No evidence that I'd been drinking at all …

How could I be so irresponsible? What the hell was I thinking, inviting a man over with my teenage daughter across the hall?

"Go, Lanie. Go to your room. I'll wake him up and ask him to leave."

When she didn't budge, I raised my voice a few octaves: "You have school in the morning. Now, go!"

The hurt expression on her face came and went so quickly, I almost wondered if I'd imagined it.

"Screw you," she huffed, then turned and walked out of the room. She slammed my bedroom door behind her.

In the silence of my bedroom, I crept over to the window and sat down on my favorite reading bench that over-looked our suburban street. It was almost morning, the dark mountain ridges in the distance tipped with dusty browns and burgundy reds.

How long has it been since I watched the sun rise?

When Delanie was young, she loved the outdoors. But I was still with her father then, Michael. Most of my memories of her early years were corrupted by memories of fights with Michael and sleepless nights as I thought about Dillan.

Here's the thing: when you bring a baby home from the hospital, you're supposed to be happy. "It's a miracle that one of the twins survived," the doctor had told me. "At least you have Delanie," my friends had told me.

But having a beautiful baby girl didn't make me any less sad about the son I'd lost. The room with blue borders I'd never use, and the drawers of blankets and onesies I'd picked out specifically for him ... no, those things couldn't be forgotten, even if I did love Delanie with all my heart.

Michael left us when Delanie was five. He didn't go far. Less than two miles from here, he lived with his new wife, Samantha, and baby son, Braxton, in a Victorian mansion they had restored. Delanie had a room there—she *loved* that room—and she visited them every other weekend.

Apparently, Michael's not verbally abusive with his new family, and he gave up drinking years ago ... how convenient for them.

The drinking and the dating ... I'd only started that recently, with the nudging insistence of my two best friends. It seemed good for me—*healthy, even*—but incidents like this couldn't happen. I had no recollection of what happened last night, or who this strange man was. This went way beyond normal socializing ... I'd obviously blacked out and lost control.

I scanned the street below. My Rav 4 was parked at the curb in front of our house, as usual. A navy-blue Camaro was parked behind it. I didn't recognize it as belonging to one of my neighbors.

Well, at least this mystery man drives a nice car. That's better than the last guy I went out with. He didn't have his own car, or steady employment.

If only I could remember who he was or what we did last night …

"Excuse me." Sighing, I tiptoed over to the bed.

I poked his shoulder, and when he didn't budge, I pushed the blankets away from his face. "I need you to go. I don't mean to be rude … but I think I had too much to drink last night. I don't usually let guys stay overnight. And my daughter … well, she has school in the morning. So, can you please head home?"

But the strange man didn't respond. No breathy snores, not even a slight twitch. No movement, whatsoever …

"Excuse me!" I knew I was being a bitch, but I didn't care. My daughter had just discovered a strange man in my bed. My daughter who was already troubled enough to begin with …

Since joining the site, I'd invited a few men over, but only when Delanie was at her dad's. Inviting a stranger from the internet to my house on a school night while Delanie was home … well, that was totally out of character for me.

But ever since I'd started dating and drinking, I'd stopped acting like myself.

Suddenly, it's like I'm a teenager again, wild and free ... a side of me I'd long since tried to forget.

I need this man out of my bed ... and now.

I placed both hands on his chest and gave him a sturdy shake. "I need you to wake up, please."

When he didn't react, I gripped the plain white sheet in my fist and tugged.

"Jesus!" I leapt back from the bed, covering my mouth and nose.

The stranger was completely naked, but that wasn't the shocking part. It was the dark-purple stain in the center of his abdomen.

And beneath him ...

"Oh. Oh ..." The floor beneath my feet became watery and strange, the walls spinning like a tilt-o-whirl. My backside made sharp contact with the dresser, and a picture fell to the floor, as I tried to scoot as far away from the bed as possible ...

Covering my mouth so I wouldn't scream and alert Delanie, I tiptoed like a ballerina back over to the edge of the bed.

Above my bed was a ceiling fan. It was turned off, but I pulled on the light string to illuminate him better.

I bit down on my own hand, muffling a scream.

The stranger's face looked peaceful enough, his eyes and mouth closed as though he were sleeping. His hands lay flat at his sides. But he was rigid, *too rigid* ... almost like he was laying inside a casket instead of my bed.

It might as well be a casket ... *because he's dead as fuck*, I realized in horror.

I bit down harder on my hand, my body trembling in fear.

Holding my breath, I moved in as close as I dared, studying the wound. It was a hole above his belly button, jagged and red, with a dry purple stain blooming out like a flower around it. Dry streaks of blood stained both sides of his waist from where he'd bled out in the bed beside me.

The sheet beneath him was stained dark red with blood, so red it was almost purple.

So much blood! It had probably soaked all the way through the mattress and box springs.

There was blood on my side too.

Realization sinking in, I looked down at my own blue nightdress.

No way would I have let a man see me in this old, worn-out gown. So, why am I wearing it? Something about this doesn't make sense.

How the hell did he get here? Who is this man?!

Tentatively, I dabbed at a big, crusty stain on the side of my gown. The color of the gown was too dark to tell, but I knew without a doubt it was blood.

His blood.

He was bleeding in the bed beside me ... and I had no idea.

Placing my hand over my mouth again, I gagged on vomit tickling at the back of my throat.

How the hell did he get here in the first place?

And, most importantly, how did he wind up dead?